# The Wolf's Mate Book 2:

## Linus & The Angel

R. E. Butler

ISBN: 1492201480
ISBN-13: 978-1492201489

# DEDICATION

To my husband B.B., and to B.L., whose support gives me wings. A special thanks to Jackie G and Amanda Pederick - thank you for being my friends, my beta-readers, and my confidants.

# CONTENTS

# ACKNOWLEDGMENTS

Cover Artist: Ramona Lockwood

A special thanks to Lisa at Editors Cove for editing this book for me. Thank you for your kind words and support!

# CHAPTER ONE

Linus was woken from sleep by the buzz of his cell as it danced across the nightstand next to his bed, sounding like an out-of-control woodpecker. He blinked the sleep from his eyes and picked up the phone, his eyes barely registering the alarm clock that read 2:17. *Shit, it was early.*

He should have checked the display, because he wouldn't have answered it if he'd known it was her.

"Linus!" Brenda whined. "Linus, I need a ride."

He sighed and sat up, swinging his feet down to the carpet. "It's fucking late, Brenda."

"But there was a blizzard, Linus, and I don't want to get trapped at this guy's house for days."

His sluggish brain picked up on part of that. "Wait, are you on a date, and you're fucking calling me for a ride? You have got to be kidding me, Brenda. That's low even for you."

Her voice tipped whinier, "But you're my husband."

"Not any more. We've been divorced for three years. This has to stop. Just don't fucking call me anymore."

He hung up and sat staring at his cell phone while she proceeded to call him four more times and leave voicemails, emails, and texts. He finally turned it off. In one of the kitchen drawers, he found the paperwork for his cell plan and called the 24-hour customer service number to have his number disconnected and exchanged for a new one. As he sat at the computer to send a message to the pack about his new number, he also decided it was a must to get a new email address, so he did that first and then sent all the new information out to everyone. Except his ex. He was sure to get a ribbing from the pack, especially Jason the alpha, on what a whipped puppy he'd been the last three years for her. Six months ago, he would have gone running to rescue her and then begged her for sex.

But three months ago he watched Jason finally claim his rightful mate in the hybrid-wolf Cadence. They'd grown up together and it had been a hot mess for years. Finally she realized what he meant to her, what it meant to all of them, and they'd become truemates, taking her rightful place as his alpha mate. That didn't technically have anything to do with him, since he was only fourth ranked in the Tressel Pack. But because of some other shit with Cadence, their pack had to handle the next in line alpha of the Garra Pack. The Garra Pack had shared their small town of Allen, Kentucky, and it was their next in line alpha who had to be handled, because he wanted to claim Cadence as his own.

When it came right down to it, Linus had let Brenda walk all over him because he wanted her back. She was completely human and he was completely wolf, but he'd loved her enough to marry her, or at least he thought he loved her. Was it really love if it wasn't reciprocated? They hadn't even made it a year. She refused to be around the wolves, accused his friends of trying to sleep with her, and then in the end she'd threatened to leave him if he didn't turn his back on the pack.

She was what the others called a Chew Toy, and he'd broken the cardinal rule of wolves: you don't marry the girls that just wanted to fuck the big bad. He'd helped her pack, given her money for her own place, and hell, he'd sat by the phone waiting for her to call and want to come home. And she did, sometimes. When she needed something or when she had an itch that needed scratched.

But this was it. He was done with Brenda, done with that part of his life, and now, he was tired as hell but restless and couldn't even think about going back to sleep. Oblivious to it while he'd slept, a storm had blanketed their town with a few feet of snow. He was very glad he'd gone to the grocery yesterday and stacked firewood in the garage.

Most of the wolves his age, which was twenty-seven, lived in a trailer park on the north side of Allen. The next generation up, their parents, lived in regular homes scattered around town. Allen was a low income, blue collar sort of southern town. There was one garage where he worked as a mechanic for Jason who owned the place, one nice restaurant, one bar, and one grocery. There was a post office, too, but it had been shut down and blended with the next town up which meant their mail was always late.

The Shrew had been too high class for the trailer park, so he'd sold his trailer to one of the younger wolves and bought a three bedroom modular home that took six weeks for the pack to build. And then she left. He'd wanted to sell it, but Jason had convinced him to keep it and just get rid of everything that made him think of her. He he did a thorough housecleaning six months ago, and this was the first time he'd heard from her since then. It was easier to talk to her, think of her now, since he'd watched Jason fight for his woman.

In the beginning, he'd thought he was in love with Brenda, but he could see now that he'd been foolish. She was attractive but not pretty, too thin for his normal tastes, but she'd wedged herself into his life and he'd let her. Then he didn't want to live without her. No one liked her; everyone thought he was a complete idiot for being with her, but he'd mistaken her desire to be with him because he was a wolf for real affection. Now, he vowed not to rush into the physical side of things again, because that's how he'd gotten trapped with Brenda in the first place.

Granted, he didn't want to take fourteen years to finally get another girl, the way that Jason and Cadence had danced around each other since they were children, each too chicken to admit that they craved the other. They were hard to be around, even now, because they couldn't keep their hands off each other, and they didn't care if it was public or not. During get-togethers at his home, he'd walked in on them a dozen times in one of the spare bedrooms. He tried not to be jealous – wolves were notoriously horny creatures – but he couldn't help it. Seriously, if he wasn't having sex in his own house, than no one else should have sex in it either.

It just wasn't fair. He wanted a woman that he could lose himself in like Jason did with Cades. A woman that only wanted him, only loved him – not because he was a wolf, not because of anything else he had to offer, but just because she loved him.

He shook his head at his own pipe dream and decided to go for a run. If there was a woman like that out there for him, she certainly wasn't anywhere he'd looked. He stripped at the sliding back door and tried not to let too much snow in when he opened it, crossed onto the deck, and shut it, shifting as fast as possible.

He shook the snow off his dark gray coat and was glad he wasn't prone to getting chilled in his wolf form. It was easy enough to let his mind go to his beast, like turning the faucet from cold to hot. He took in the scent of the fresh snow, the cold air, and the smell of the woods outside his back door. Leaping over the snow draped stairs from the deck, he landed with a fluff of snow before darting off into the woods.

He just ran, darting between trees, leaping easily over fallen logs and low brush. The woods at night in the snow. Was there anything better to a wolf?

He lazily chased a small herd of deer, just for fun. He had no intention of taking one down, although he could easily. In the leanest winter months they were on the thin side, and their meat would not be as succulently tender as it would be in another two or three months as they fattened themselves up in the spring. He'd rather wait, thanks.

On and on he ran, changing directions for no reason, not really running anywhere in particular, just totally digging letting his wolf free. And then two distinct scents caught his nose. He skidded to a stop to scent them better. One was canine, not wolf, and one was human. It was far too cold for a human to be out. Worry and curiosity hit him at the same time, and he took off for the scents, running at top speed.

He crested a small clearing and found what looked like a snow-covered body lying near the bank of a frozen creek. At this point, he was a few miles from his home. He nuzzled the forms and found them to be a woman, alive, and a dog, dead.

She didn't rouse when he nudged her harder, so he shifted to his human form, prayed she didn't wake up and freak out that he was nude, jerked her stiff body into his arms, and took off for home. He'd never run so fast in his human form in his life, and his heart pounded in his ears as he closed the distance to his home as quickly as possible. There was something about her that he couldn't put his finger on, but he desperately wanted her to live.

Nearly frozen himself, he dropped her on the couch and began to pull off the clothes that were frozen to her body. Her lips were blue, her face dead white, but she was breathing in a shallow way and that was good. *Right?*

His hands shook and ached as he pried off her thick coat and threw it aside, tossing her ice-caked tennis shoes and socks as well. He couldn't get her jeans off, so he darted to the kitchen and came back with shears, carefully cutting the material up one leg and then the other, peeling it from her before he made quick work of her sweater. She started to shiver, tremors rocking her petite body, and he pressed the back of his hand to her panties and found them wet and frozen, too. He put aside his thoughts of her modesty and cut them off along with her bra and wrapped her in a blanket from the couch.

With his comforter and two other blankets on top of her, he kicked up the heat, trying not to bite off his own tongue with his chattering teeth, and he started the fire that had long died in the fireplace. Within ten minutes, the fire was roaring while he pulled the mattress from his bedroom into the family room and moved her from the couch to the mattress.

"I'm really sorry, sweetheart, but, naked's best and I'm still a fucking icicle." Maneuvering under the blankets, he curled her into himself, finding her slightly warmer than freezing, and he shuddered against her as the fire slowly warmed them both.

He had a thought that he should call his mother, see if there was anything he should do for her besides just warm her up; but he was too sleepy to do anything except absorb the warmth of the fire and take in the scent of the woman in his arms that had suddenly come to mean everything to him.

He slept for hours, waking often as she warmed up and started to move, making small, whimpering sounds of pain. He checked her fingers and toes, secretly delighted to see they were painted cherry red, and they were miraculously safe from frostbite thanks to her insulated gloves and socks. He wondered how she'd ended up on her side in the snow with that dead dog but hadn't found any injuries on her.

He woke up with a soft leg sliding over his and drawing him close. His cock had been hard for hours, ever since it had thawed, but he'd pushed aside his thoughts of the unconscious woman in his arms as much as possible.

But this...was an interesting development.

Her short nails abraded his back, and she drew him close to her heat with her foot on his lower back.

He wasn't sure if he was still dreaming or if she was dreaming, but he sure liked the scent of her arousal, the way her mouth moved across his shoulder, and the soft panting of her breath. She smelled incredible, like vanilla and heat, woman and nature combined. Seeing her in the daylight had revealed an incredible beauty, and his body had not missed the opportunity to respond, even as inappropriate as the circumstances were.

"It's okay, sweet; let me get you something to drink." He whispered for no reason other than he didn't want to freak her out if she was still asleep.

She hummed in her throat, and it went straight to his cock. "No, don't go. You smell so good." She slid one hand from around his back between them and grasped his cock at the base, spreading her legs further apart and attempting to draw him inside her. Which is exactly where he wanted to be. For like eternity.

"You're still asleep." He cautioned but couldn't bring himself to extract his cock from her grip, and his words sounded almost pleading in their tone.

Her eyes flashed open, and he was greeted with the warmest brown eyes he'd ever seen in his life, surrounded by thick lashes like lacey fringe. "Make love to me, please, I want you to."

Angling herself slightly closer, his cock brushed the wetness of her body, and he would have been helpless to stop himself if he'd had a brain cell actively working in his head at that moment. She moved her hand back around to his lower back, pulled him towards her, and tilted her face up for a kiss. He gave it to her, sliding his tongue into her hot mouth as his cock slid into her more-than-ready body.

Groaning at the tight heat of her flesh as it fought him with delicious pressure, he thrust in completely and stopped, her gasp of pleasure into his mouth a chanting prayer of thanks and pleasure. Cradling her against him, he took her mouth while his body staked a claim to hers in the most primal of ways until her whimpers of pleasure and thrashing head drew his wolf to the front of his brain.

Never a presence like this before, his beast seemed captivated with the beauty in his arms, and the desire to mark her rose so heavily in his mind that he growled, and the sound spilled out of his throat while he licked her neck and bit down gently, enough to bruise but not enough to bleed and mark permanently.

"Oh, yes, yes!"  She cried, digging her nails into his shoulder and drawing blood, the actions making him thrust into her harder, faster, and she met his frantic movements with her own, her hips in perfect sync with his.  All thought was gone, there was only feeling, only heat, only her.

*Mine.  Mine.  Mine.*

For the first time, his thoughts were not his own but his wolf's as well, feral and needy with the desire to keep her forever.  *I will kill anyone that touches her*, he vowed to himself, and his wolf growled in agreement.

# CHAPTER TWO

Karly groaned. Everything ached. Badly. She tried to get up, but there was something heavy across her stomach. Lifting her head, she took in a quick breath at the sight in front of her. A very naked man was cuddled just under her breasts with one of his legs thrown over hers. And she was also naked.

Seemed like this was a situation that should make her freak out, but she was feeling pretty content. So what happened? She chewed on her lip and tried to remember the last thing she could.

*Oh, hell.*

She'd chased her neighbor's little rat terrier out into the snow because she was worried he'd die. She'd chased him forever. Stupid little dog.

And something happened?

Right. She fell and was overwhelmed by the cold and snow.

Her brain whirled and images crashed around. She had vague notions of being nudged by something furry and then carried and then gradually warm and safe. She knew that feeling. This man, who had obviously saved her life and, according to her aching pussy, had allowed her to ravage him in thanks, was a werewolf.

Her breath caught in her chest, and she could have cried. She'd found her mate! Her fifteen months of searching and apparent near-death had brought him to her. What the hell were the odds of that happening? Fate's a funny thing, for sure.

Incredibly warm under his weight, she let herself go into the sweet heaviness of him and listened to the sound of his breathing. She wished his face was turned up so she could see him, but knew it wouldn't matter. Her nature had picked him, and he would be perfect for her and she would be perfect for him. An instant connection as old as time, wolves and their mates.

She closed her eyes, and her mind drifted back to when she found out what she was, at age twelve. Raised in a wolf pack by her human mother and werewolf father, who was second in rank, she was taught everything there was to know about wolf packs even though she wasn't a wolf. At that time their pack, the Soualit Pack from West Virginia, had forty-five wolves who lived and worked mostly in the small town of Brink's Pond. On her twelfth birthday, her mother told her to sit down at the kitchen table and take off her shirt. There was a woman there she didn't know who had drawings all over her arms and neck, what Karly came to find out were called tattoos. She had a tray of little jars and instruments and was snapping blue surgical gloves on her hands.

"This is Caledonia. She is going to give you the mark of our heritage, my daughter. You must accept this burden of pain in order to begin your journey." She turned and pulled off her own shirt, and when she swept her hair to the side, on her right shoulder blade were three black tattooed symbols. One sort of looked like a tree with two branches, one like a house with an antenna, and one like an upside down v. The tree and house were together and there was a small space and then the v. The tattoo couldn't have been more than two inches wide and about that high, but it stood out starkly on her skin. Karly couldn't remember if she'd ever seen it before.

Her mother's delicately long fingers touched her shoulder. "This is the symbol of our people, our kind. It is the mark of the Angel family line, the Ancient Greek symbol for Soul Mate. That is what the women in our family are born to be. Mates for werewolves."

She sat down in front of her and took Karly's hands in hers. "Do you accept the mark of our people? Do you accept that you are an Angel, a human woman born to find your one true werewolf mate?" Her eyes were sincere, her sweet smile warm and patient. Karly had always expected she would marry a wolf someday, it's all she'd ever known after all, but to know that she was somehow made to be one particular werewolf's mate was an incredible knowledge, and it filled her with warmth.

"Yes, Mom."

Her eyes shone. "Then do not cry, daughter. The pain will last for only a little while, and then you will bear the mark for the rest of your life. Let me tell you all about our family so that you can begin to prepare." She sat down in the chair next to Karly, and Caledonia had taken up the needle after prepping her skin and asked her to tell her when she was ready. Karly took a deep breath and said she was ready, and Caledonia touched the needle to her skin. Karly thought it would hurt badly, it was a handful of needles moving very fast and pushing black ink into her skin, after all. But it was more of an annoying sort of mild pain, and when she relaxed enough after the first pass of needles into the design she had sketched, then she could focus on her mother and their history.

Her mother's middle name was Angel and so was Karly's. The reason was so that no Angel Mate ever forgot what she was. When the Creator made the first werewolf, he was a ravening thing, more animal than man. So the Creator made a woman for the wolf, who was sensitive to the wolf's nature and could soothe him like no other woman alive could. He made a perfect mate for him. The legend went that the wolf had been in his shift, cutting a path of destruction through civilization like a thresher through wheat, when he spied the woman. Intent on killing her, he looked into her eyes and felt his heart beating for the first time.

The werewolf shifted back into his human form and took her for his mate. He called her his angel, his salvation, and that was what she called herself from then on. When they had children, the boys all became werewolves, and the girls all became soul mates, ready at age twenty-one to find their mate-for-life. Entirely human but genetically supernatural, the girls had the ability to soothe their mates. Supercharged by the gene pool of their ancestors, any male children they had were almost always powerful wolves, and the females became the next generation of Angel Mates.

She knew this was true: her three brothers were all alphas of packs in North America. Bren in Ontario, Rico in Washington, and Graise in southern Florida. She was the only girl.

When the tattoo was done she had learned so much about her ancestors and was thrilled to know that in nine short years she might be able to find her mate. No one knew if the journey would be easy or difficult, but it was always perfect. The joining of the angel and the wolf was almost instantaneous, even if they were strangers, because his beast recognized what she was immediately, even if the human part of the man didn't.

Karly worked hard to graduate early from high school and finished her bachelor's degree just a month before she turned twenty-one. She had hoped on some level that her mate would be found within her father's pack, but it didn't happen. When she turned of-age, none of the unmated males that she had grown up with were her mate, which meant she had to start her journey.

After turning twenty-one, she took a month to prepare herself to leave home, and thanks to her father's personal wealth, she never wanted these months for anything except her mate. Armed with a new car, a map of the known wolf packs within North America, and a fully stuffed bank account, she left her home pack and began a journey. All she needed to do was find the place where the wolves hung out and settle down for a few weeks. If her mate was in the town, she'd be drawn to him and him to her, and if not, she moved on.

The first few months were most difficult, because she missed her family and grew discouraged very quickly. She talked to her mom every night, and she bolstered her hopes that she'd find him eventually. But she had to take on the search and keep going.

As the first year of her travels began to draw to a close, she started to grow weary of being alone. It wasn't just her mate that she was missing and hoping every day she would meet, it was the constant moving. Every two or three weeks, she would have to pack up her life and go somewhere else and start all over again. She went north first, while it was still summer, moving steadily up the coastline until the cold drove her south. The map was full of red Xs from packs she'd visited. There were just so many. Smaller states had usually two or three packs, larger states could have a half dozen or more. It varied, depending a lot on the packs themselves and whether they were friendly or not.

She dated as she moved around. She was no prude, and it wasn't as if she was trying to save herself or anything. Hell, she hadn't been a virgin since she was fifteen, and although she'd rather not think about The Prick, at one time he'd been her best friend since they were children and part of the pack. Sometimes you think you know someone and then they go nuttier than a squirrel. Life was sucky like that sometimes.

Now, fifteen months later, she wasn't even sure how she wound up in this part of nothing Kentucky. She'd been unable to find a place to rent short-term in the town of Allen where the pack resided, so she'd had to go to the next town over, North Paddock. Not the nicest place she'd ever lived, but it was clean and relatively safe. And in the south, most of the packs stayed away from the very big cities, so you tended to get the odd rental room in a grandmotherly sort's home or sometimes small complexes like hers. But that would change now. She could call her mom and share the news, and then she could put down roots finally. At age twenty-two, this angel was going to spread her wings for the first time and start her life fresh.

All her internalizing had woken her up enough that she really needed to pee. She looked out the large windows of what looked like a family room, and the sky was dark. She wasn't sure what that meant and couldn't see a clock anywhere, but when nature called, you gotta answer, that was for sure.

She tried to slide out from underneath him so she didn't wake him up, but he was like a very hot dead weight on top of her. She tickled her nails down his ribcage as far as she could reach, and he gave a snorting laugh and jerked off her, surprise coloring his face.

*My, my.* "Hello, handsome." She smiled, not bothering to try to cover herself. He'd gotten the whole show after all.

He smiled like he hadn't smiled in a very long time and wasn't sure how and finally, after staring at her for a long moment, cleared his throat and said, "Hello."

"Bathroom?"

Looking like he'd forgotten something, he jumped up. "Oh, shit. Sorry." He held his hand out for her and pulled her up gently.

"Why are you sorry?" She followed him out of the family room down a short hallway.

He cleared his throat again and looked sheepish, "I wanted to wake up before you, and be, you know, dressed? So you didn't freak out." As if she wouldn't know that they'd had sex. At least once but probably more, considering the stickiness between her legs.

Before she could even think of a response to that, they were in what looked like a master bedroom that someone had taken a wrecking ball to and stopped in front of an open door in the far wall.

He left her standing and rushed around in the bathroom and the bedroom for a minute and then said with a slight pant, "There are fresh towels on the counter and a long shirt. I don't know how you feel about wearing my shorts, but I put a pair in there for you and a pair of sweatpants."

"Are my clothes not dry? I could wait." She chewed her lip, glancing past him into the small bathroom.

"Um," he looked uncomfortable, "I had to cut them off. They were frozen to you."

Damn it. She liked those jeans. But she'd rather be alive than dead with those jeans intact, so she guessed it was a wash. "Thank you, um, I don't know your name. If you told me, I've forgotten. My name is Karly." Hello embarrassment. What a fantastic story for their grandchildren.

"It's alright, Karly. We really didn't…do much talking, so I don't expect you to remember everything. My name is Linus Mayfield. I'll go make us some breakfast. Take your time, call if you need anything." He looked like he wanted to give her a kiss or something, but before she could close the distance to him, he grabbed some clothes out of the closet and took his cute butt out the door.

She shut the bathroom door and used the toilet. While the hot water got going in the shower, she looked at herself in the mirror and gasped in shock. Hickeys ran up and down the length of her neck and there were bite sized bruises on her shoulders and down the meat of her biceps. She checked her neck carefully and didn't see the tell-tale four dots that indicated he had marked her as a mate. Wolves were twitchy about marking, and a wolf that marked a woman without a discussion would be upset with himself. Unless they were psychos, of course.

She marveled at the feelings inside her. Her heart beat soundly in her chest, blooming with first love. And her body was singing for him. Like, literally. If they hadn't just officially met, she would have called him for some hot shower sex. She was disappointed that their first time together was missing from her memory. She must have been really out of it from the cold, but her body knew what to do regardless.

The hot water coursed over her, the pressure hard enough that it stung at first, but she welcomed the feeling after a while and used his generically male products. He clearly didn't have a girlfriend that stayed over, or he would have had the tell-tale bottle of floral body wash. She was very glad for that news. All he had was a bottle of V05 shampoo and a bar of soap that smelled like Irish Spring. You could tell a man's sex habits by checking two places: the fridge and the shower. If he had any sort of feminine bath products in the bathroom or wine coolers in the fridge, then he was used to overnight guests of the female variety.

She used his hairbrush and the hairdryer she found underneath the counter to dry her shoulder length black hair. She wondered if Linus liked the way she looked as she pondered her reflection. She was short and curvy with her mother's pixie features and a mixture of her mother's ivory skin and her father's Egyptian olive coloring, so she had a nice year-round tan.

She looked at the boxer briefs with a smile. At least they weren't tightie-whities. She put them on, and the sweatpants, which were twice as long as her short legs but at least had a drawstring. She rolled the bottoms until her feet, in his white socks, peeked out, and then she held up the long sleeved t-shirt that advertised a garage called Pete's. It looked well worn, so perhaps he worked there. Without a bra, her generous breasts threatened to split the fabric, but there wasn't exactly anything she could do about that. And he already knew what they looked like. And felt like. And tasted like, considering her aching nipples. She allowed herself a moment to blush at her wantonness, and another moment to yell at her brain for being unable to recall what they were like together.

Vague memories poked in her mind, and she scanned through them. She could hear herself asking him to take her. Pushing when he offered to leave. He had growled, more than once. She could guess what she'd been thinking when she woke up in his arms, safe and alive – that she was glad that he'd saved her and that she'd known even subconsciously that he was hers. And she was lonely. Achingly lonely. And tired of searching.

How do you start a conversation that changes everything? *Hey, Linus. Thanks for saving my life and what I'm sure was plenty of hot sex. By the way, I'm your truemate, and we're perfect for each other. So when can I move in here?*

Somehow that seemed crass. Perhaps she didn't need to say anything. He would know that they were mates, and if he hadn't figured it out yet, then he'd figure it out pretty soon and then she could tell him everything.

When she came out of the bathroom, she found the bed put back together and the room straightened. He must have been working furiously fast while she was cleaning up. The smell of bacon assaulted her nose as she walked out towards the kitchen that was attached to the family room they had woken up in and found him standing at the stove in jeans and a black t-shirt. His hair was damp, so he clearly had another bathroom in his house and had taken a quick shower. Or she had taken a damn long one.

He turned as if he could sense she'd come into the kitchen and gave her a smile. "Have a seat." He gestured with a fork to the table that was set for two. Coffee in a pot on a coaster, milk and sugar, orange juice in small glasses. *Adorable.*

She poured a cup of coffee for herself and fixed it with milk and sugar. "Thank you, Linus. For saving my life."

"I'm glad I found you. I hope breakfast for dinner is okay, I don't do too much cooking. I'm mostly a grill kind of guy." He smiled again and turned back to the stove.

"Breakfast is great, thanks."

She took the quiet to peruse the man that had gotten to know her so well physically without knowing more than her name. Tall, over six feet, with broad shoulders and a narrow waist that spoke of good genes and discipline. Muscular but lean, a perfect combination. Strong jaw, straight nose, and powder blue eyes. She'd never seen eyes quite that color. So light, so pretty. His dark brown hair was short and tousled, the perfect length for grabbing and holding onto. She mentally patted her angel nature for picking out such a perfectly handsome man.

It was damn hard not to think about sex around him. He looked like a man that didn't know how sexy he was, and that made him even more irresistible. She tried to think of other things except him, so that her body didn't start smelling like a horny teenager, but that didn't work. Instead she concentrated on remembering the lyrics to Henry the Eighth. By the time she got to the tenth verse, he came to the table with a bowl of scrambled eggs with melted cheese, slices of thick cinnamon raisin toast, and crispy bacon.

As he sat down, she said, "So it's 8:30 at night, but it's still Friday, right? I didn't lose a whole day, did I?"

"Yeah, it's Friday. I found you around 1:30, maybe, by Fischer's Creek."

"That's good." It had been 12:30 on Friday when her neighbor, Mrs. Beckinson, had banged on her door and begged her to help find little Jacques.

"Was the dog yours?" he asked, a sad look on his face.

"No. Dead, right?"

He nodded. She told him the story, and he laughed at her self-deprecating humor. Only an idiot would run out into a blizzard to find a dog that had nipped and growled at her on more than one occasion.

She looked out through the back sliding glass door to the snow that lay piled up high on the deck. "Is it pretty bad out there?"

He looked disappointed for a second but then his face shifted to neutral, "City's on lockdown for the next twenty-four hours at least, maybe forty-eight, depending on how fast Damsen can get their streets plowed and come here. Are you, do you have someone you need to call?"

Aw, was that his roundabout way of asking if she had a boyfriend? "No, I live alone, and my parents are in West Virginia. I don't want to intrude on your life, Linus."

He snorted and took a bite of his eggs. "I don't have much of a life, Karly, and that's the damn truth. You're the most exciting person to cross my doorstep, ever. I'm sorry if you're ashamed of what happened between us. I won't," he sighed low and dropped his eyes, "I won't touch you again, I promise."

She tapped her fork on the table until he looked at her. "Don't be rash."

"But, I don't want you to think that I, well, it wasn't," he stuttered and floundered, and his face flushed a most adorable crimson. She'd never seen a shy wolf before. It was pretty easy to guess that he'd been burned before and was twitchy about probably everything about women.

"Linus, Linus," She put her fork down and reached over for his free hand and squeezed it, wanting to comfort him, "it's okay. I mean, I'm a little mortified because I didn't remember your name, but I feel safe with you. And I'm not ashamed, I promise. I mean, unless you have a girlfriend or wife?"

His eyes narrowed just slightly, "Ex-wife, no girlfriend."

"Good. Well, I'm single, too," *painfully single*, "and judging from all my hickeys and my aching joints, I'm guessing we had lots of fun. Next time around I'd like to remember, okay?" She flashed a grin at him, and he laughed, the tension easing from his shoulders and his lips breaking into a smile.

"Okay." He smiled. Sweetheart. Funny, shy wolf.

The quiet stretched for a few minutes while they ate, and then he put his fork down suddenly. "I have to tell you something, and if I don't, I'm going to hate myself."

She put her fork down and folded her hands and waited, giving him an encouraging smile.

"I'm a werewolf." He said the words like they hurt his mouth. As if she might freak out at the mere thought. "You're safe with me, I swear I won't hurt you or anything, I just, I can't pretend I'm human because I'm not entirely. And if you thought I was, I didn't want you to think I kept it from you on purpose."

He ran both hands through his hair as if it were a nervous habit and then peeked up at her through the veil of his thick lashes, those baby blues imploring her to be kind. Whoever had hurt him was going to pay if she ever saw them again.

"I knew you were a wolf when I woke up."

Confusion reigned. "You did?"

She took a moment to decide if she should tell him exactly what she was, but he probably wouldn't know the history of her people; it wasn't a story that got told around the campfire much anymore. In fact, a lot of the wolf packs she ran into thought it was just legend. "My father is second of his wolf pack."

He straightened. "Your mother is human, though, right? Because you don't smell like a wolf to me."

"Yes," she smiled, "she's human." *Sort of.* "What do I smell like to you?"

"Vanilla." He blushed again, and she felt warm from head to foot. When he met her eyes again, the heat banked in the depths told her that he was feeling the connection to her as strongly as she was. With some difficulty, he picked up his fork again, "Please tell me about yourself, Karly."

"Well, I'm twenty-two, I'll be twenty-three in the fall, and I have three brothers, and a fine arts degree, and I like to paint and take photos and be creative. And I just moved to North Paddock less than two weeks ago."

"Why did you come here, for a job?"

*I came to find you.* "I've been doing a bit of traveling, trying to find my place in the world. There was a guy in my father's pack that kind of flipped out and got a little possessive of me, and I knew he wasn't the right man for me, so I decided to head out on my own."

He looked surprised. "How long have you been traveling?"

"Fifteen months, give or take."

"Because he couldn't take a hint?"

"Not just because of him, because there wasn't anyone in my father's pack that I wanted to be with, and I didn't want to stay when there were other places for me to explore."

He hummed in his throat, looking disappointed. "So you won't be sticking around, then?"

Aw. Where was his self-esteem? "Actually, I plan to stay." He brightened considerably and then she used his own questions on him. Age twenty-seven, he was fourth ranked in the pack that was led by his close friend and his mate who was close to her age. They were mated from childhood but had some problems getting to the place they were now, but he didn't seem to want to dwell on them, and that was okay with her. He skipped his childhood and went right to the meat of his romantic history which was apparently very short: married for less than a year to a wolf groupie and that ended three years ago.

"Do you miss her?"

He shook his head. "No, I miss the time I lost pining for her, and I hate that I will have to tell the woman I want to spend the rest of my life with that she's not the only wife, you know? I feel like I've already betrayed her." He looked away, leaning back in his chair.

What do you say to that declaration? He clearly had spent a lot of time beating himself up over his choices. Everyone had laundry lists of regrets. Since they were both done eating, she skipped saying anything to what he'd said because nothing she could say would change how he felt about himself at the moment. She knew all about feeling dirty and used because of a former lover, but he didn't need her empathy right now, and he wouldn't necessarily understand her willingness to ignore his past. All she cared about was their present right now and the future.

She stood and picked up her plate. "Thanks for breakfast. Let me do the dishes for you."

He stood up and made a grab for her plate. "You don't need to do the dishes; it was my pleasure to cook for you."

He seemed insistent that she sit back down and relax, but she followed him anyway. He flipped on the faucet, and she stood next to him, leaning against the counter with her hip against the cabinet. He was concentrating very hard on the water from the faucet, as if it were pure gold flowing from the silver hardware.

She turned off the water. He turned, and she looked up into his pretty eyes. She undid the button of his jeans and said, "Dishes can wait, Linus."

His eyes went wide, and he paused long enough that she had a mini panic attack. "Oh, crap. Was it not good? You don't want to?" Her mouth went completely dry, and she thought she might curl into a ball. She'd never had complaints before, but then she hadn't ever really asked.

He jerked like she had hit him and growled, putting both hands on her shoulders. "It was incredible, Karly, I feel like I can't get enough of you and I don't want to scare you."

"Not scared. Want you." She breathed in deeply, and the very male scent of him washed over her, warming her body. She hadn't realized she closed her eyes until she heard him take a deep breath and growl very softly in the back of his throat. She opened them slowly, and his eyes were hooded, his mouth parted slightly, and the expression on his face was pure bliss.

His hands slid slowly across her shoulders to her neck, his fingers playing on either side. His mouth lowered in slow motion to hers until their lips met and their tongues slid together, deep and searching. One of his hands slid around to her waist, and he lifted her off the ground as if she weighed nothing. She wrapped her legs around his waist. She tried to climb inside him through his mouth while he moved them through the house and rolled her underneath him on the bed.

He spread her legs with his knees and straightened his arms so that his fists were buried in the mattress on either side of her head. She didn't expect the frown. "What's wrong?"

"I don't have any condoms. I'm not exactly that guy, but I damn sure wish I was right now."

"I'm on the shot."

His frown disappeared in a heartbeat with a sweet smile that morphed into a look so full of lust that she thought her insides were going to melt. "You look damn sexy in my clothes, Karly. Better out of them, though."

"Must be something you can do about that, my sweet wolf."

Their clothes disappeared in a flurry, and she got an excellent look at his magnificent body before he slipped down hers and spread her thighs apart with two very large, warm hands. He swirled his tongue around her clit, and she grabbed onto the wooden slats of the headboard while he feasted on her as if she were the most exquisite thing he'd ever tasted in his life.

Linus played her like an instrument, searching for all her spots and finding them, driving her to climax again and again.

She writhed under his hands while he tongued her core, lapping at her juices with throaty growls, "Linus, please!" She cried out when the shiver of the last fingers of the climax had worked through her, fairly sure she couldn't have another orgasm if her life depended on it.

He licked his lips, swiping his finger across his mouth and sucking her wetness from it. With liquid grace, he slid up her body, and she grabbed his waist with her legs. He may have planned to enter her slowly, but she dropped her hands from the headboard and dug her nails into his butt, pulling him inside at the same time as she thrust her hips up to meet his.

"Holy fuck," he ground out, a shudder weaving through him. She breathed out a laugh, only because she was pretty sure that his cock was so big that he was poking her lungs and she couldn't form any words. He kissed her for a long time while he moved slowly in and out of her, cradling her against him and caressing every inch of skin he could get his hands on. And then by slow degrees, he lost hold of his control and pounded into her until he drove her to another plateau of pleasure that she had never reached before. Stars winked behind her eyes. She felt him spasm inside her, and he said her name when he came. It was the sweetest sound she had ever heard.

They made love several more times over the course of the night — on the bed, on the couch, in the shower. And every time they were together, it strengthened the connection between them until it was like they'd known each other forever. Somehow she thought that was really how it was between angels and their wolves. Because it was ancient, and powerful, and sweet. To realize that someone was made for you, waiting for you. It was a wonderful thing.

She passed out across him like a blanket well after first light, numb from her eyebrows down to her toes and deliciously aching. She'd never been happier in her life.

# CHAPTER THREE

He held his little sweetheart on his chest while she dozed off after their sex marathon that started Friday night. Now, it was late Sunday morning, and he'd never been so incredibly worn out or felt so amazingly connected to a woman in his life. She was his mate. He'd never been so sure of anything else in his life. Already he could see how different it felt when it was a true match and not forced the way he'd done things in the past. Because he was lonely and didn't want to wait, he'd rushed forward and ended up hurting everyone.

Karly. Karolyn Angel Nylock. Gorgeous. Sweet. Funny. Perfect. His. Oh, yeah. His wolf was not about to let him let her get away. His fangs had elongated so many times while they'd fucked around the house that his gums ached. No, that's not right. Not fucked. It hadn't been fucking with her, it was love. He'd actually made love with her. It might be new love, but he knew himself well enough to know that in no time he was going to be head over heels for her, and he'd give his eye teeth to park his mouth between her thighs for the rest of his life.

Everything was different. She didn't lie there passively while he did all the work; she gave as good as she got, passion in every action. She'd spent a great deal of time after the second time they were together, tracing every muscle in his body with her fingers and then her tongue, and he'd had no choice but to do it back to her. It had felt amazing to have someone pay such careful attention to him. He knew he wasn't bad looking — he'd turned heads over the years, and his chest and abs were hard-won from the gym. The girls in the bar would swoon over his muscular upper body, but it wasn't like this. It was like she was trying to memorize each line, to touch every part of him.

And he'd damned well enjoyed doing it back to her. Ex-fucking-squisite. She had great tits and the most sensitive nipples he'd ever encountered. She had ticklish spots on her hip bones and the back of her knees, and her feet were sensitive enough that when he bit gently on her instep she just about came. And he loved her red painted toenails. So sexy.

As he drifted off to sleep with her curled into his chest the way he wanted to go to sleep the rest of his life, he couldn't have been happier. He'd finally found the woman of his dreams, and he wasn't going to let anyone get between them. His wolf in agreement, he hugged her slightly tighter, closer, and fell asleep, a humming growl of contentment the last thing he heard.

"Yo, dude! Where are you?"

*Shit!* Linus lurched from the bed as his brain tried to register the voice coming down the hallway. It wasn't Michael, no it couldn't be. No, no, no! He slammed the bedroom door shut and met Michael and Bo, second and third in the pack, coming down the hallway. Michael put his hand up to cover his eyes.

"Fuck, man, put some clothes on."

He growled and put his hands over his cock. "What the hell are you guys doing here?"

Bo quirked his brow at him. "Better question is why you didn't answer your cell. Jason's been trying to get hold of you for a few hours."

"I've been busy."

"Oh?" Michael peered over his shoulder like he could see through the door. Linus bristled, and his wolf stood at attention. No. No fucking way was Karly going to be around them. She. Belonged. To. Him.

"Guys," he ground out, "is there something that Jason needs or did you just come here to bust my chops?"

Michael seemed to sense something was going on, and he wasn't exactly the kind of guy that walked away from causing trouble. Bo was, though, and he stepped in. "It's nothing we can't handle. Plows are due to come out today, and Jason wanted you to drive for a shift, but we can handle it. Since you're busy."

"Yeah, I am. Thanks for taking my turn."

"You can owe us," Michael quipped. Linus knew he would. He corralled them back to the front room and away from his sweetheart and watched them shift on the back porch and take off with pants between their jaws. He locked the sliding door. If he'd left it locked they wouldn't have gotten in, wouldn't have been on their way back to the bedroom where his mate was lying naked. He wasn't sure what he would have done if they'd come into the room, but he was feeling out of sorts and possessive suddenly. Angry.

Then just as quickly as it came over him, it seeped away, and he felt more in control and calm. Karly had put her arm around his waist, coming to stand next to him at the back door. And she was wearing his shirt again, which he loved. "You need to go?"

"Nah. You hungry, sweetheart?"

"Sure. But let me give it a try this time."

He followed her into the kitchen. "I like cooking for you, Karly." Truth. He liked it a great deal. Maybe because she appreciated it. Maybe because she didn't expect it or act like it was his job.

"Well, I'm not helpless in the kitchen. I do have some skills."

He gave her a teasing smile. "So you're not just another pretty face?"

"Gosh, I hope not."

"Alright." He put his hands up in a jest of defeat. "If you want to cook so badly, have at it. But I'm very picky," he teased, and her brown eyes danced. Turning her sweet face up for a kiss, he gave her one and then another and would have kept going except she gave him a gentle shove and reminded him he was naked.

It was just after lunchtime, so they hadn't gotten more than a few hours of sleep. Not that he cared. He liked being exhausted like this. He hated the knowledge that with the plows starting the roads would most likely be cleared by morning, which meant he'd have to take her home and then go to work, and the bliss that he'd known since 1:30 a.m. Friday morning was going to stop.

Donning a pair of track pants and nothing else, he wandered back into the kitchen and watched her drop a sandwich carefully into a bowl, turn it, and then put it on the stove on a hot pan. She peered up at him. "Monte Cristo."

"Never had one before." He joined her at the stove where four sandwiches were now frying. It was amazing that she knew how much he could eat. Wolves put food away like there was no tomorrow and a chance of a food shortage. He'd dated women over the years that complained about it, or thought it was funny, but she took it all in stride.

"So your dad's pack?" He brushed a lock of hair from her shoulder. "Are they like old-school with traditions and stuff or more modern?"

"Definitely old-school. The pack alpha has been in power for, well, longer than I've been alive, and he runs things pretty strictly. Pack's on the small side, all family groups, and they don't let newcomers in unless it's through a mating."

Her father was second of the pack. Her mother was something called a caretaker, which was an older term for someone that handled the cooking for the pack. It was a position of honor in some packs, and Karly's pack had four of them.

They didn't have a caretaker in their pack; it wasn't something that they'd ever had. Granted, he never really paid much attention to the traditions when he was a kid, because he didn't think it would matter. When Jason's father Peter was alpha, he was powerful but kind, and let the wolves have more freedom than a lot of packs that ran them like monarchies, and some of them even sequestered themselves in towns with no humans at all. As long as the pack members didn't cause trouble for each other or the humans, showed up on the full moon and for meetings, then Peter never really cared what else they did. Work where you want. Live where you want. Jason was much the same way, maybe even more lenient because of his youth. But from past experience, he was also very serious about the job and would not shy away from leading and delivering pack justice or punishment if the situation warranted it.

"So in your pack, then, everyone eats together?" He found the whole thing very cool.

"Something like that. On the weekends, definitely. The alpha's house is like a big gathering place, and there's always food to eat in the kitchen and a meal on the table at six like clockwork every night, but it's not mandatory. He uses the weekend meals for his top ranked and their families. It doesn't sound like your pack at all."

She helped her mother cook for the pack for years. She went to public school until eighth grade and then was home-schooled online for high school, graduating early and starting right away with college courses.

He set the table for her, and by the time she joined him, he had a feast on his table that he couldn't believe actually came from his own kitchen. Besides the sandwiches, she had made a pot of potato chowder, a loaf of bread with melted cheese on it, and a pitcher of iced tea. He was in complete awe.

"I would have done something for dessert, but I wasn't sure what kind of stuff you like. I'll make something later. Is this okay?" She looked at him with those big brown eyes. He could see that she really wanted him to be happy with what she had done.

"Holy hell, Karly, this is amazing. You didn't have to do so much for me."

She raised her brow. "Why wouldn't I?"

Indeed. He tucked into the food and was unprepared for how amazing everything was. The girl could cook, that's for damn sure. Immediately he thought about the empty restaurant in town. Lonestar. At one time it had belonged to the father of their alpha female, Cadence, a horrible human that hated wolves because his wife had been killed by a rival pack female while she was pregnant with Cadence. Somehow, the attack made Cadence into the odd hybrid that she was but had put a permanent chip on his shoulder about their kind.

When all the shit went down in October over Cadence and the pack that had shared their town for many decades, the Garra Pack, the entire pack had pulled up stakes and hit the road, leaving the bar and restaurant in town without anyone to run them. Just recently, they had tentatively taken on a DJ to play weekends at the bar known as Jake's. Jake had been the alpha of the other pack. They were all hopeful that the DJ might want to run the bar for them, too, but he seemed reluctant at the moment to do anything except play music.

"Have you ever thought about going into the restaurant business?" he asked, after polishing off the second sandwich.

She gave him an incredulous look. "My stuff's not that good."

"Are you kidding? You are a fantastic cook, Karly. No kidding. If you do your art stuff better than this, well, then I don't know why you're not in a museum somewhere."

She blushed, and it was adorable. "You know you don't have to sweet talk me to get me into bed."

He laughed. "I would anyway."

They spent the rest of the afternoon talking, sitting on the couch and getting to know each other. By the time dinner rolled around, Karly had made herself at home in his small kitchen, and he loved watching her. He could actually see in his mind's eye what their life might be like together. He could picture her waiting for him after work, eating dinner together. He could even see her sweet little flat belly rounded out with his child. Now that was something he craved on a cellular level.

Unfortunately, the call came about ten that Jason expected them at the shop in the morning because the pack had gotten the roads cleared to town. He didn't want his little bubble to burst.

While they made love before bed that night, he kept stopping himself from saying a dozen things that ran through his mind like an errant freight train.

*I love you.*

*Move in with me.*

*Marry me.*

*Park on my face for about a week.*

But he stopped himself, mostly by biting his tongue, which eventually started bleeding. Damn sharp fangs. He was afraid to rush her but afraid to let her go. He wanted to mark her and drive down to one of those cheesy quick stop marriage places in Tennessee tomorrow. Confusion reigned in his mind, at least for those moments when he could actually think straight. He was running on pure awe and instinct with his little sweetheart. Willing, feisty, as insatiable as he'd ever hoped for a woman to be in his bed.

And now, blissed out, drenched in sweat and other sweeter things, he loved the sigh from her mouth as she cuddled into him. "You're wonderful, Linus," she yawned, "and very good at wearing me out."

He chuckled. "I would prefer that they hadn't gotten the snowplows so soon."

"Real world beckons."

He bit the inside of his cheek to stop himself from asking her to move in for the hundredth time. Instead he smoothed his hand over her shoulder. "This is a damn sexy tattoo, you rebel. What's it mean?"

"Soul mate." She yawned again, rubbing her cheek across the small patch of dark hair on his chest, unable to keep her eyes open.

His wolf sat up. She was someone's soul mate? He'd slaughter him. Whoever the hell he was. "Is it from someone in your past?"

"No," her voice started to slur, "I'm your angel, Linus. Yours." She sighed deeply and fell asleep.

Angel? Something pricked at the back of his mind. It sounded familiar. But at least she said she was his. That was enough to pet down the hackles on his wolf so he didn't go stalking off into the snow to find someone who had her heart. He wanted it for himself. Maybe that made him a selfish bastard, but he didn't care at this point. He'd wandered across her in the snow, and maybe it was fate, but he damn sure wasn't going to let her go. The last thought he had as he drifted off to sleep was that he'd seen that symbol somewhere else, when he was young.

# CHAPTER FOUR

Karly really didn't want to get up. She wasn't feeling lazy; she just liked sleeping next to Linus. He was so warm, like a personal space heater, and with his arms around her, she felt perfect and safe and complete. It was a nice feeling. And all the sex was a good bonus, too. But they couldn't stay snow-bound forever.

He slept soundly underneath her while the sky outside the bedroom window was still dark and the clock read a too-early 4:47. She debated staying right there and waiting for him to wake up or getting up and making him breakfast. Her better nature of wanting to take care of her mate had her sliding slowly off him and out of bed and pulling on the shirt and shorts that had mostly been off of her for the last two days. She shut the bedroom door so he could rest. He mentioned the night before that he was supposed to report to the garage at eight so she figured he should be up around six maybe, which gave her an hour to feed him right.

Fortunately, his pantry and fridge were well stocked, along with a large chest freezer in the garage that he kept stockpiled with meat. He was obviously used to having some of the pack over in the summer for cook-outs. She whipped up a sausage and egg casserole and popped it in the oven then made a quick loaf of banana bread. She heard the door open just before six followed by his yawn that had become very familiar. He came out of the bedroom already showered, in jeans, a short sleeved shirt with Pete's Garage in faded blue script across the front, his hair still damp.

"Good morning, beautiful," He kissed the top of her head and put his arm around her.

"Morning."

"Have you been up long?"

"Not too long."

"You know, a guy could get used to all this special treatment. It's not really fair." He groused, and when she looked up at him, she could see the unhappiness in his eyes even though he was trying to joke about it.

"You deserve to be treated special. I made coffee, have a seat."

"Yes, dear," he laughed with another kiss and squeeze before going to the table. She pulled the casserole out of the oven where she had been keeping it warm and put it on the table, along with a plate of the sliced bread.

"I don't know how you keep putting this stuff together. I didn't think I had the ingredients to make half the stuff you've made for us."

She served him a big wedge of the casserole and took a square for herself. "Just experience, I guess." She blushed slightly. She wasn't used to all the compliments. In her father's pack, the caretakers were supposed to be good cooks or they weren't going to be doing the job much longer. You didn't get praised for doing your job.

"So what will you do today?" he asked, tucking into the food.

"I don't know, actually. My car is probably buried behind a snow plow drift in the parking lot, so going somewhere is out of the question, not that I had anywhere to go, anyway." She felt like she was babbling and going to say something stupid, like begging him to let her stay at his house for the day. To wait for him to come home from work, to make him dinner and take care of him.

"Can I see you, uh, after work?"

He looked like he thought she would say no. Silly wolf. "I'd like that."

He finished everything, declaring it incredible and delicious. She finished eating before him and pulled on his socks and sweats. They left as soon as he was finished eating, and he carried her out to his pick-up truck in the garage even though she had shoes. She saw his motorcycle in the garage, and he said that the whole pack rode and he was looking forward to riding with her once the weather got nice. She wasn't certain that he even realized that he was talking about them in a future way, and she didn't point it out, even though she found it sweet and wonderful.

As expected, her parking lot had been plowed in a way that blocked all the vehicles behind a tall wall of snow with only sidewalk-sized holes leading to the units. He pulled up in front of her unit and frowned. "You live here?"

"Yeah. I wasn't looking for a long-term place, and there aren't really that many places to rent in this area."

He gave her a long look. "This place isn't exactly safe, Karly."

Shrugging, she reached for the door handle. His hand tightened on her arm. "Wait, you act like it's not a big deal if the place is safe or not."

"It's okay. I've lived in better places, but I've lived in worse places, too. I told you, I don't usually stick around more than a few weeks in any one place, and sometimes the short term places are iffy."

"Why is that, again?" His baby blues narrowed.

She sighed. "Because I was looking for a reason to stay, and I didn't find one before."

He was full-on frowning by this point, so she pointed to the clock on the dash. "You're going to be very late if I don't get going, Linus. And then the lunch I made you will have gone to waste." He'd been thrilled that she packed him a lunch. She'd been looking for black pepper and saw a small cooler and packed him a few sandwiches and some other things.

"I'm not done being unhappy about this place," he said finally and got out of the truck. He came around to her side, opened the door, and pulled her into his arms.

She didn't know what to say to that, so she said nothing. She liked that he was concerned about her, but it wasn't as if she had a choice. Allen did not have any available short-term rentals. She unlocked the door, and he carried her inside, kicking it shut with his foot and putting her down. He was practically glaring at her.

"Linus?" She ran her hands around his waist, hooked them at the small of his back, and leaned into him. He sighed and put his arms around her. "I'm sorry, Karly. My wolf is like snapping in my brain about leaving you here."

"That's sweet. I'll be fine. I've been fine. You should get going. I don't want your boss to hate me before he ever meets me."

He looked down at her and she could see the war in his eyes. "Yeah. I'll see you about six, okay, angel?"

Her heart stopped. "Angel?"

He smiled, the action splitting his lush lips. "Last night you said you were my angel just before you passed out. It was sweet."

Holy hells bells! He kissed her once on the lips, and she was almost too stunned to react to it. Gathering her wits, she said goodbye and shut the door behind him. What were they talking about that she said she was his angel? She scanned her mind for last night's events and couldn't remember anything after collapsing on his chest. She must have been half asleep.

Well, clearly he hadn't heard the old legends or he would have put the two together; his wolf's concern for her and her being an angel. So tonight she would tell him. She had her bound history books with her. Along with her two bags, the box of books was the only thing she carted from place to place. She would show him her history, her place in the Angel line, and explain the significance of their connection together. What she'd learned over the weekend was that he had been hurt so badly by his ex that he was gun-shy about relationships. Worried to rush, worried not to rush, constantly doubting himself. And he clearly didn't think he was worth very much, thought there were other men, wolves, who were better than him.

The problem was that packs like his were getting further and further away from traditions. It wasn't about taking away a pack's freedom to make their own choices, it was about holding on to what made them special and great. It sounded like their full moon gatherings were more about partying and hanging out than communing. When she took him back to her father's pack to get married, he would get to see what he called an old-school pack work. She'd seen a lot of packs. Some very traditional, stiflingly so, and some so loosely grouped together that except for the fact they all shifted on the full moon, there wasn't anything tying them to each other. Was there a way that was better over the others? In her mind, yes. And truly any children that she had with her mate, she would want them brought up learning the traditions and culture of their heritage. If Linus had been taught properly, he would have known what she was right away, because his wolf would have recognized her. And he wouldn't be second-guessing himself, which was clearly what he was doing.

Last night, when they made love before bed, he kept starting to ask her things, and then he would stop abruptly. That fear — that little bit of brokenness — endeared him to her but also made her a little nuts. It would have been a lot easier if she didn't have to explain this whole thing to him. Not that she would trade her travels for anything, though.

Her mom never left her birth-pack. Her father, either. When he came of age, he knew that she was going to be his. When she turned twenty-one several years later and that connection solidified, they had waited for each other. Maybe Karly didn't wait to have sex because she'd known subconsciously that none of the men in her father's pack were going to be hers, she didn't know. In the long run, it really didn't matter. Linus was hers now, and they'd be together forever.

Picking up the phone, she dialed her mom who would be done with the breakfast dishes by now. As the phone rang, Karly could picture her bustling around the kitchen as she cleaned. Her mother taught her to take pride in her work and to always do the best job, even if it was a lowly job like washing dishes or sweeping the floor. Everything that made up the home was important because the pack was important. Pack and home were words that were interchangeable in the world she'd grown up in.

"I found him, Mom!" she gushed as soon as she answered her cell.

"You did? How wonderful! Tell me everything." She heard the sound of liquid pouring, the clink of a spoon, and the creak of wood. Her mom sat down with a cup of coffee to listen to her, as if she was still home. Karly did the same as she shared the story with her, making a small pot for herself and sitting at the two person table in the efficiency kitchen.

She told her about nearly dying and being rescued, her embarrassing wantonness and not remembering his name but then making up for it, and the weekend that Linus and she spent together. She and her mother had an open relationship. Although her mother would have preferred her to remain a virgin until she met her mate, she had armed her with the knowledge to protect herself both physically and emotionally and helped her have a strong sense of self-worth.

"And he's fourth?"

"Yeah. He's the sweetest, most shy wolf I've ever met."

"He sounds perfect for you, darling, but of course he would be. It's a shame that his pack has lost the traditions by modernizing. It's what the alpha believes is pretty much the fate of many packs now. Younger alphas want more freedom and less responsibility, so they abandon the very things that make them unique."

Karly agreed wholeheartedly. "I'll tell him everything tonight. If he needs some time to come to terms with it, then I'll give that to him. But I could tell he was on the verge of telling me he loved me and asking me to move in with him. He just didn't understand that I already belong to him."

"Your father will be thrilled your wandering days are over."

She snorted lightly. "He'll be thrilled? I've been on the road for over a year. I just can't wait to settle and put down roots."

"I'll send word to your brothers. We'll plan for you to come out for a visit in the spring when the weather clears. We can plan the wedding then."

"Sounds good to me." Although some might consider that things were moving too fast, Karly knew from what she'd witnessed over the years that once wolves found their mates, they really didn't care to waste time to make them theirs forever.

"Take care then, my daughter, and call if you need anything."

Karly hung up and finished her coffee. As she rinsed off her mug and put it in the dishwasher, there was a knock at the door, and her neighbor's shrill voice came through the door, "Did I see you come home, Karly? It's Lola. I brought muffins."

Sweet, lonely Mrs. Beckinson. Karly would buy her a new puppy to replace Jacques. It completely escaped Karly's attention that she was probably worried all weekend. She opened the door, and Mrs.

Beckinson hugged her with one arm, holding a small muffin tin in a hot pad with the other. She smiled at Karly, and her eyes crinkled at the corners before she started to cry. Karly pulled her gently inside and shut the door, leading her to the kitchen table.

"I'm so sorry, Mrs. B. I found him, but I slipped on ice and fell and passed out from the cold. A man happened to be out and he rescued me, but Jacques was already gone. I'm not even sure where it happened, but I can ask my friend if he can remember so we can find him and give him a proper burial."

She wept quietly. Widowed, no kids, and living in a week-to-week place because the mortgage on the home she shared with her husband for thirty years had ballooned at the end and she lost it right after he died. That little rat dog was all she had in the world.

"I'd like that, dear. I was so worried about you. I never thought you might get hurt out there, but when you didn't come home, I didn't know what to think. Where did you stay?"

"The man that found me, his name is Linus. He lives in Allen, and he saved my life. I stayed with him for the weekend and I'm so sorry you worried. I would have called if I had my cell phone with me or knew your number by memory." She made another pot of coffee, knowing that her morning was now shot because she wouldn't leave until after lunch at least. But Karly could plan her dinner for Linus. Six o'clock couldn't come fast enough.

Mrs. Beckinson told her stories about her little dog while they ate her homemade blueberry cream cheese muffins. She was an excellent baker, and she and her husband had run a successful catering company for years. He was the driving force behind it, and she was just the "pretty cook". Now she lived off her pension and sold baked goods at flea markets in the summer.

Karly shifted the topic slightly and told her about Linus while Mrs. B. swooned over her romantic good luck. She was one of those women who read a lot of romance novels. She believed in the knight in shining armor rescuing the damsel in distress and then plowing her for days afterwards. Not that there was anything wrong with that. It's pretty much what happened to Karly.

Karly made cold-cut sandwiches for them, and then Mrs. B. left, leaving two muffins. Karly had already made meat sauce while she visited and made a pan of baked ziti, a loaf of white bread and put a salad together. After she cleaned the small place, which was little more than a front room, kitchen, bedroom and bathroom, she took a shower and got ready.

Choosing her outfit carefully, she dressed in a short, dark blue wrap dress that gave her good cleavage. She left off the stockings and put on a navy blue satin bra. Feeling daring, she skipped the panties entirely and slid into a pair of wedge heels. The table was set, candles were lit all over the place, and soft music played from the romantic music channel on the television hanging over the gas fireplace which was quietly burning. Her nerves were a jangling mess as she looked over the small place, her eyes falling again and again to the leather bound book that marked her as the last Angel of her family's line, at least until she had a daughter to carry on the traditions of their people.

When the knock on the door sounded just after six, her heart leapt into her throat and stayed there. What if he ran away? What if he thought she had lied to him? What if he needed time to come to terms with what she was, what they were together? What if his ex burned him too badly for him to recover?

With trembling hands, she reached for the door.

# CHAPTER FIVE

He sat in his truck outside her tiny apartment for several minutes after he dropped her off. He wanted to go back up there, tell her to pack and take her back home. He didn't like this place. He didn't like that she lived outside Allen. He didn't like it at all.

Tonight, he told himself as he put the truck in drive and headed to work. "Tonight I'll tell her that she's my mate and I want her to move into my house," he said aloud. It sounded right, good, and his wolf growled in agreement. If she bucked at it, he would give her the master and take the spare bedroom himself and promise to stay away from her until she was ready, but he couldn't help himself from wanting to know she was safe. It wasn't just the incredible sex; it was the amazing connection he felt to her. Nothing had ever felt so right before. Her scent, her laugh, her eyes. All of it was as if she'd been carved to perfection just for him.

"You're late," Jason said from behind the counter. "I'd think you would want to be on my good side, considering."

He tucked the cooler under his arm and stomped the packed snow from his boots on the rug. He wasn't *that* late. "Considering what?"

"Considering you didn't return my calls all weekend or show up for your plow shift. What was so important that you ignored all your duties?" Jason pushed his blonde hair away from his face and gave him a narrowed, unhappy look.

"I had company, Jason. I didn't even hear my cell, or I would have answered. It wasn't until Bo and Michael showed up that I even knew that you'd made plans for the pack to help out with the plow trucks." Plus, he'd turned off his cell because Brenda had been calling him so often, and clearly, he'd not turned it back on after he got the new number.

"Please tell me that you're not getting back with Brenda, Linus. If you passed on pack business for her, I'll skin you alive." The look in his eyes said he meant it, literally.

"No, it wasn't her, Jason. I did meet someone, but it wasn't Brenda. I cut ties with her this weekend, completely."

Jason's eyes narrowed further. "And this someone is human?"

"Yes."

He scoffed disdainfully. "Do you have something against wolves?"

His wolf sat up, and it was all he could do to not growl at his alpha. Jason wouldn't take that lightly, and he'd wind up with a shiner or busted lip and a bruised ego. He didn't want to get into a fight with Jason. Not today. "I don't, Jason, but this girl is different. And I'm not really interested in talking about her right now. I didn't shirk my duties because of her, it was unintentional."

He moved further away from the counter towards the back, and Jason gave him another long look. "Yeah, well, see that it doesn't happen again."

He nodded and walked away, putting the cooler down on his work bench. He was dying to see what she'd packed for him, but he was trying to wait until lunchtime so he could be surprised. He was surprised enough as it was. She'd gotten up to make him breakfast and cleaned the kitchen faster and better than he ever could, and then she'd managed to make him lunch, too. He was toast. He was absolutely head over heels for his angel, and that terrified him on several levels.

"Hey, dick," Michael gave him a friendly punch in the arm. He looked tired. "Hope she was worth you pulling my tow truck duties for the next two weeks."

So that's what Michael thought was worth him taking an extra snowplow shift? Could have been worse. Michael was a complete smart ass. That was about the sum total of his personality.

"Thanks, man," he said finally.

"So when can I meet her?" He leaned his elbow on the workbench and looked at the cooler. Linus tucked it under the workbench where he could keep an eye on it. He'd rip throats out if anyone touched it. No one touched what was his. Not anymore.

He tried to evade the question, grabbing a few tools and turning to the bike he'd been in the process of tuning up before the storm. "What makes you think there's anyone?"

"Well, first off, your whole place smells like sex. But other than that? You were naked and angry about the interruption. Unless you were just saluting your own sailor, there." Michael smirked and folded his arms.

Linus sighed. "She's, well, it's a long story, and I'm not really interested in talking about her right now. When I am, I'll let you know."

"Fine, fine." Michael put his hands up. "Just so you know, Jason is righteously pissed at you for ducking his calls. If all you have to do is tow truck duty, you'll be lucky. He's always relied on you to be there when he needs you." He watched Jason's back. True. Linus was the most reliable of the top ranked. But he wasn't some faithful lap dog, and the whole thing made him bristle.

Michael went to his own work bench and began to work. A few months ago, Michael would have pestered him until he was blue in the face, and

Linus would have either had to spill his guts or punch him in the teeth. Lately, though, ever since Jason and Cadence had hooked up, Michael had started thinking about his lack of a love life. Hell, all of them had. Sometimes you see a couple that's right together, and it makes you crazy for what you're lacking in your own life.

As he toyed with the wrench in his hand, he wondered how he could have ever thought all that misery with Brenda had been love of any sort. He'd been miserable the whole time they were together and then worse afterwards. She'd sucked all the life out of him. His thoughts turned to Karly, and his whole body warmed. She was just exactly what he'd wanted his whole life but had been too caught up in trying to force himself to see it in other women. None of the pack females ever did it for him. Maybe it was because they'd all been around the block with every other male in their age group and he didn't really like sharing. Except of course for Cadence, who he had never slept with, but she hadn't technically been pack or really a true wolf. Then there was her shadow Callie, but Callie was so weak in the pack she was almost human anyway. Other than friendships with those two females, and theirs was weak to start with, he'd never had serious feelings for anyone. Ever. Karly was like a breath of fresh air on a stifling, humid day. A sunrise after a restless night. The ocean at your feet.

He realized he'd been daydreaming and staring at the wall when someone snapped their fingers in front of his face. It was Bo. "There's a call for you, man."

He straightened. "Thanks, man."

"Yeah, well, thanks for having clothes on." Bo grinned at him and Linus sighed. He would never live that down. At least his cock hadn't been hard at the time. That was something to be thankful for. As he walked to the front to get the phone, he had a thought that it might be Karly, and he couldn't stop the joy that leapt into his heart.

Expertly dashed, his heart deflated instantly at his mother's voice,

"Linus, I need you to stop at your grandmother's tonight. Her kitchen sink is backed up again."

"I've got plans tonight, Mom. Can't she call someone?"

"She did call someone. You."

He groaned inwardly. He would not get out of this for anything less than a disaster requiring hospitalization. His mother Joyce, all five feet of her, was a force to be reckoned with. Feisty and fiercely protective of her family, she was not the sort of woman to take no for an answer. She'd been highly ranked with the females of her day and held that position with pride.

He didn't want to be late for Karly. As it was, he was going to have to take a short lunch to make up for coming in late and then book it right at 4:30 so he could grab a quick shower and change. He didn't want to go to her place covered in grease.

"Okay, tell her I'll come by at lunch today."

There was a slight pause. "It's not that horrible woman is it, Linus? I swear, I will give you such a beating if you're back with her. I'm not joking."

Hanging his head, he growled internally. Would no one let him forget anything that he'd done? "Mom, it's not her. I'm done with Brenda. I'll –" the front door swung open and a customer walked in. "I'll talk to you later, okay? I need to go."

As his mother said goodbye and he hung up, Cadence walked out from the back office to greet the customer. Jason had hired her to do the bookkeeping and run the front, and she was a natural. Tough enough to deal with the bikers that came in for repairs and mods on their bikes yet sweet enough to charm even the crustiest old lady who wanted a discount for being distantly related to someone that worked there. He gave a nod to her, and she smiled back.

He figured he could go help his grandmother and then eat. He didn't dare take more than a half hour break, or he'd have Jason on his ass. Throwing himself into his work, he tried not to daydream about Karly, but it was damn hard. She'd just permeated his entire being. He could still smell her on his skin, could still feel the press of her mouth against his when they'd said goodbye this morning, and if any of the guys in the shop could see into his head, they'd get a show that would rival any of the porn he'd seen over the last few months.

Lunch couldn't come fast enough. He clocked out and grabbed the cooler, not wanting to leave it unattended at the shop. He was thrilled with the prospect of seeing what she'd done for him; he knew it would be perfect.

His grandparents lived in a small neighborhood in the center of town. Their tiny two-bedroom house had been a haven for him as a child. He loved his mother a great deal, but his father had been a genuine asshole and had not treated him or his mother very well. As an only child, he'd grown up trying to protect her and gotten knocked around good for it. He hadn't been sorry when his father took off with a younger female and left them high and dry, even though his mother had been devastated.

He was there in two minutes. He gave his grandmother, Gladys, a hug when she opened the door. She was as small as his mother but no less dangerous if she was pissed. His grandfather Eugene had arthritis in his hands. Medicine didn't really help wolves, and the pain had gotten bad enough that when he shifted on the full moon he could barely walk. It was unusual for wolves to get those sorts of illnesses as they aged; they stayed fairly healthy for the span of their lives, but it did happen occasionally. In his grandfather's case, he had gotten caught in a hunter's trap when he was a young man, and it had snapped over both his forelegs. As he aged, the damage turned into problems for his mobility.

"Hey Pops," he called to the front room, hearing the sound of the television.

He heard the replying grunt and knew that was as much as he'd get for now. "I can't stay to chat, grandma, I'll fix the sink and head back."

"I was going to make you lunch." She put her hands on her hips as he pulled the toolbox from the counter to the floor and opened the cabinets under the sink.

He couldn't stop his smile. "I already have lunch taken care of."

"Oh?" She smiled, her gray eyes crinkling with the motion.

"Yeah, I met this girl over the weekend." He pulled the wrench out and put it on the pipe after securing a bowl to catch the water. "She made me lunch."

"That's sweet."

Sweet wasn't quite a strong enough word for it, but he didn't elaborate. He worked quietly and quickly. In the mess that came out of the pipe as he poked the back end of the wrench into it, he heard a clinking noise and fished out her wedding ring. He handed it to her, put the pipes back together, and dumped the black water out onto the snow in the backyard.

"I wondered where that went." She laughed and washed it off and he cringed, worried she was going to drop it again. Already ten minutes had passed. He needed to get going.

"I need to take off, grandma."

"Wait, I have something for you." She hurried out of the kitchen, and he growled to himself but sat down dutifully at the table. The daily crossword in the paper that she did faithfully was laid out, and he picked up the pen and began to doodle in the margin, staring out the back window into the woods that lined the development.

"Here," she handed him a pair of dress slacks. He'd completely forgotten about them. Before Christmas, he had been invited to Jason and Cadence's reception and they were his only pair. When he went to put them on, there was a gaping hole in the pocket so he'd dropped them off and worn his nicest pair of jeans instead but had not bothered to get them.

"Thanks, grandma." Perfect. He could wear them tonight. He stood and kissed her cheek.

"Who do you know that's an Angel?" she asked, fingering the design he'd absently drawn in the corner of the newspaper.

"What?" He wasn't sure he hadn't heard wrong.

She pointed to the three symbols he'd sketched from memory, the tattoo on Karly's right shoulder. He'd noticed it when he had made love to her while she was on her hands and knees. He'd grabbed hold of her hair and pulled her up, and she'd screamed his name in pleasure. He had kissed that mark, bitten it, and licked it, all while he'd pounded into her.

"That mark is the symbol of the Angel Mates."

He blinked. Angel Mates? Why did that sound familiar? She slapped the back of his head, "Didn't you ever listen to the stories I used to tell you about our heritage, our people?"

"I'm not sure I follow." He rubbed his head. Time hadn't made her strength lapse at all.

"The Angel Mates are half breeds, but not like Cadence. They are as supernatural as we are...the product of their angel mother and their wolf father." He must have looked as confused as he felt because she gestured to the chair and he sat down mutely. She joined him across the small table and folded her hands together. "The story goes that when the first werewolf was created that he was more beast than man.

So the creator made a woman for him, his perfect mate. She was made for him alone, could calm his beast, brought out both his nurturing side and his protective nature. Their children were both. The females were mates for wolves and the males were full blooded wolves. Each generation of angels is the same. They always have the middle name of Angel to remember their heritage, and this tattoo is marked on their skin around the age of twelve. They grow up in their home pack, learning the ways of our people, their future mate, and when they come of age, they begin to search for their mate. Sometimes the mate is within their home pack, but often, their journey is long and they move from pack to pack, searching. The connection is supposed to be primal, instant. Like love at first sight but stronger."

"So the females are angels, like real angels?" He could feel the color draining from his face as he tried to reconcile what his grandmother was telling him. Karly's middle name was Angel. She had the tattoo. She called herself his angel when she was nearly asleep. She'd been traveling for over a year, moving from place to place because she hadn't found a reason to settle down.

She clucked her tongue at him. "No, not like a heavenly angel. It's supposed to be the term that the first wolf used. You don't remember the story?"

"I don't know." He frowned.

"He was in pain, miserable from shifting and unable to control his beast. She appeared to him and calmed him. He called her his angel, his salvation."

"I thought that a human-wolf child would always be human. How could the male children be wolves?"

"Because the angels aren't human, not any more than we are. What makes them what they are makes that possible. So, tell me, Linus, where did you see this symbol."

"On the right shoulder of the woman that I'm sure is my mate." He swallowed hard. He stood up, and the chair clattered backwards. He righted it, his hands shaking, and said, "I need to get back."

She followed him to the front door. "Linus, if you feel like she's your mate, then she is. Did she not tell you what she is?"

He shook his head. His mouth felt like he'd swallowed sand. She hummed in her throat but said nothing. He kissed her cheek, called out a goodbye to his grandfather, and beat feet back to his truck. He shot through town as fast as he dared on the slightly icy streets and carried the cooler back to his workbench. He just barely made it back in his thirty minutes. Just barely.

Resting his hands on the workbench, he stared at the cooler. Was it possible? He thought the angels were a myth. The legends about their kind were often exaggerated from generation to generation, and in their current pack, no one talked about the legends at all. The curse of the modern packs that were streamlined into human society and not hiding what they were as they did in the past meant that a lot of the traditions and history weren't passed down like they should be.

He opened the cooler slowly. A folded piece of paper was lying on top, and he opened it. In delicate script, she'd written:

*I can promise I miss you already. K.*

A part of him wanted to be angry. He'd been feeling all weekend that she was his mate, and he was afraid to scare her off with the strength of his feelings. But she clearly already knew they were mates, so why hadn't she said something to him?

Just as quickly as it appeared, his anger seeped away. He knew why. She didn't want to scare *him* off. He'd been more open and honest with her than any other person in his life to date, and he'd told her everything that had happened between him and Brenda, and his past relationships besides her. She had looked at him with both compassion and pity. He'd hated that look, the pity. He was certain she thought he was gun-shy about relationships and was probably just waiting for him to realize what she was to him. He couldn't be mad at her. He loved her. He knew that was as true as the fact that the sun would set tonight and rise tomorrow.

4:30 couldn't come fast enough. He ate and worked on the bike, ignoring the chatter around him. He needed the time to think over how he would tell her he knew the truth. That it had been in the back of his mind all weekend.

The lunch was incredible. Even more than the food, was the thought that went into it, and now he understood why she'd wanted to take care of him. Because mates did that for each other. Apparently, even Angels. The cooler was filled to the brim with food. Three chicken salad sandwiches, a thermos of sweet tea, and a plastic container of potato salad she'd made the night before. She had clearly kept some aside for him because he'd practically licked the bowl clean it was so good. And tucked inside a napkin were two squares of walnut brownies that she'd also set aside because there hadn't been any left when he was finished.

He wanted to call her, to thank her for everything, but he realized he didn't have her phone number, hadn't even thought to get it because he had known he would see her after work. He put his head down and got back to work. It wouldn't do to be caught slacking off. Jason hadn't called for him, given him a hard time, or read him the riot act like he expected, but that didn't mean he wanted to call attention to himself. The guys in the shop with him clearly thought he was not in a good mood because they didn't talk to him much outside of work things, and that was okay. He was in a great mood, getting better with each pass of the minute hand that drew closer to him being able to see Karly. He was just damned annoyed that it was only Monday, and he'd have to go another four more work days before he could bury himself in her for two days non-stop.

*Karly. Karly. Karly. Mine. Mine. Mine.*

"Taking off?" Jason's voice stopped his hand on the front door at exactly 4:30. He clenched his jaw and turned, giving a blank face to Jason. He didn't want to give him fuel to make him stay. He had no way to communicate with Karly if he was detained, and he would hate for her to worry or think he wasn't going to show up.

"Yeah, I've got plans." He gritted his teeth against the words he just had to say, "Unless you need me to stick around."

Jason's head cocked to the side, and he looked at him carefully. For what seemed like an eternity. "You look different."

"Because I have to leave?"

Jason snorted. "No, you just look...not miserable."

He chuckled wryly. "Yeah, well, getting something you've wanted for a long time will do that to a guy, right?

Jason half smiled. "I suppose so. I was going to give you a hard time about dodging plow duty, but Michael's already saddled you for two weeks on-call. Just make sure that you don't fuck up the tow truck stuff. If you blow off even one call, you and me are going to have huge problems, new woman or not."

Linus held up the cell phone that was the direct line for tow truck calls. "I won't."

"Have a good night."

"You, too."

He barely contained his joy at the development. Jason could have caused him all sorts of problems. Racing to his house, he showered and shaved as fast as possible without causing major blood loss, tossed on the nicest shirt he owned with the slacks his grandma had repaired, and ran out the door. He planned to bring her home with him. After he told her what he'd figured out.

No, he hadn't figured it out. His grandmother had to spell it out for him like a child. He knew it now and he couldn't have been happier. His eye caught a local florist in North Paddock, a few streets away from where she was waiting, and he stopped and went inside.

The woman behind the counter smiled and straightened on the stool she was sitting on. She was older, his mother's age perhaps, with salt and pepper hair cut short and half glasses on her nose. "Hello. Can I help you find anything?"

"I'm going to see the woman I'm going to marry. I thought I should bring her flowers, maybe? But I don't know what kind."

She stood up and looked thoughtful. "Let me ask you one question: Was it love at first sight or more you were friends first and now you love her?"

"Love at first sight."

"Well, then there's only one real choice." She disappeared into the back through a swinging door. Several minutes passed and when she appeared, she was holding a purple rose. He'd never seen one like it. "This is a lavender rose called Old World. I cultivated it myself. It's rare, the color. It is used traditionally to express love at first sight, adoration. But it's expensive. I can give you a dozen in a box, for," she sighed and looked at the rose and then at him, "$120. Or I can do red for $50. I can promise you that women love flowers, period, no matter the color."

"I'll take the purple."

"Okay, give me a few minutes." She winked and disappeared.

He paced in the confines of the small shop, his wolf going crazy in his head to get to Karly. But this was a good thing to do. She deserved it. He'd been kind of crabby about leaving her at the apartment, and his beast wasn't helping his mood. And he missed her. He'd gotten a taste of heaven, and he wasn't even close to being satisfied.

She came out with a black box tied with a dark purple ribbon. When she put it on the counter, it sounded heavy on one end and she smiled, "I put a vase in for you, my treat."

He pulled out his credit card. "Thank you."

"Well," she swiped the card and punched some buttons, handing it back, "I'm a sucker for love at first sight."

He signed the receipt without looking at it, thanked her again, and took the box with him. In his truck, he caught sight of the receipt as he tucked it into his wallet, and it only read $50. Surprised but pleased, he finished the short drive to Karly's place.

Why was he so nervous? He knocked on the door, shifting the box in his arms. He felt like a teenager on a first date not a full grown man seeing the woman he loved. The door swung open, and his heart stopped in his chest and his wolf sat down and whined for the beauty in the doorway.

She was wearing a low cut dark blue dress that hugged her curves like it had been painted on, showed the top swell of her lush breasts, and barely reached the middle of her thighs that were mouth-wateringly bare. He forgot everything and just stared at her.

"Linus?" She laughed and pulled him into the apartment.

He nearly dropped the roses in an attempt to hug her and managed to hold onto them and pull her into a one-armed hug so he could feel her against him. "I fucking missed the hell out of you, Karly." He said, bending so he could put his face into her neck, worried the stinging in his eyes was going to turn to tears if he didn't get a handle on himself. It just felt so damn right to hold her.

She squeezed her arms around him tightly. "I missed you, too."

He pulled away slowly and met her willing mouth. She stepped backwards, and he mirrored her until they were in the middle of the small front room. She pushed his jacket off his shoulders, and he shifted the box of flowers in his hands as he wormed out of it and let it drop to the floor. Almost too lost in the heat of the kiss, if he hadn't wanted to hold her with both arms, he would have forgotten the flowers completely.

Reluctantly he pulled back. "These are for you."

"Oh, thank you." She blushed and took the box from him. He followed her into the tiny kitchen and watched her open the box. Her gasp and smile were enough to let him know he'd made the right choice.

She set the flowers upright on the counter in the crystal vase. There were a lot more than a dozen in there; that woman had really done him a favor. Karly turned her sweet smile to him, "They're just gorgeous, Linus, thank you."

"No, you're gorgeous."

"Such a sweetheart," her smile went even wider, and a delicious dimple marked one cheek. "So, are you hungry?"

It hadn't escaped his notice that the apartment smelled like an Italian restaurant. "Yes, but first," he hooked his finger in the center of the low neckline of the dress, right between his two favorite breasts, and jerked her to him. "I learned the most interesting thing when I was at my grandmother's this afternoon. An old legend of our people, a bit of history." He held her close and smoothed his free hand down her neck as his other hand slid down the front of her body and curved to her waist, gripping her tightly. Her pulse fluttered under his thumb. Her heart was pounding.

"Oh?"

"Hmm. It seems like my angel isn't just any angel but mine. Just mine." Her brown eyes went wide. "It's true, isn't it? It's why I wanted to mark you, why I can't stop thinking about you. You're my mate."

"Yes." Her voice was breathy.

"Are you happy about that?" What would he do if she wasn't happy?

"Of course. I couldn't have picked a better match for myself, Linus." Neither could he.

"And all your traveling?"

"I was looking for you."

"You almost died." His voice came out on a growl, and his hands spasmed reflexively on her body as the scene in the woods appeared in his mind again.

"You won't let that happen to me again."

Fucking right. "You sure as hell aren't spending another night in this place." He'd never been much of a dominant person with females, but he felt the need to make sure she was safe with him. Period.

She cocked her head to the side and squinted at him, as if she were considering it. "Well, I don't know. I kinda like this place."

He growled and didn't try to hide it as his fangs descended. She reached for his teeth and ran a finger down one canine. "Down boy. I was just teasing. Put these away until later." She laughed and kissed him, flicking her tongue along a fang, and it made his cock stand at attention, as if it hadn't already been straining the zipper ever since she opened the door. A warm hand cupped him, and he moaned into her mouth and pulled her closer. Was there anything on earth better than his woman?

He fisted her hair and pulled her away gently, and her eyes were bright. "I hope you didn't plan to get any sleep tonight, sweetheart."

"Promises, promises."

"I definitely don't make promises I don't intend to keep. Now, we need to talk, so let's eat and get you packed."

She grinned, "Yes, dear."

Another spectacular dinner later, he helped her with the dishes while they talked about her heritage. Angels were fascinating. He couldn't believe he had ever thought it was just a legend, but he was apparently not the only one or theirs the only pack that had lost hold of the traditions.

He was humbled that she'd been looking for him for over a year but also that she had been thinking about him in the abstract form of her faceless mate somewhere in the world since she was twelve. She was dedicated to finding her mate because it was her destiny. He couldn't imagine being told at age twelve that he'd meet his mate and fall head over heels for her and that would be it. She wanted everything that he did – a loving home and kids — and he wanted to give that to her in spades.

The book she shared with him about her lineage was the last book in the series that was several hundred years old. She could trace her family line back for centuries. How many people could say that? Each chapter in the book was done by the angel when she met her mate that shared details of the journey to find him, their home pack and life together, and the names of their children and the packs they joined.

"So your brothers are full wolves?"

She nodded, running her hand fondly across the last page of her mother's chapter, where her own name was written with a beautiful script and a sketch of angel wings surrounded it. "They're all alphas, actually. Bren is in Ontario, Rico is in Washington, and Graise is in southern Florida. Almost all the males born to an angel are alpha powerful."

"Are you, disappointed that I'm only fourth?"

She closed the book slowly and put it on the coffee table, turning to give him a long look. "Linus, you're my mate. You could be at the bottom, and it wouldn't change how I feel about you. You make me happy, you make me feel loved and safe and cared for, and the fact that you're gorgeous and excellent in bed are just icing on the cake for me."

He pulled her into his lap and kissed her, cupping her face to angle her mouth to his and filled her mouth with his tongue, tangling with hers while he held her tightly. He pulled back enough to lick across her lips and said, "I love you, Karly. Please be my mate."

# CHAPTER SIX

*I love you*. Her sweet wolf had just told her he loved her. The three sweetest words in the universe, just for her.

She made sure that he could see the truth in her eyes. "I love you, too, Linus. And I already am yours. Completely."

Another searing kiss that branded her soul. Another stroke of his large, warm hand. She captured his wrist as his hand started to move across the swell of her breast. "Unless you want to stay here tonight, we shouldn't get carried away."

He looked like he was considering the truth of the statement and then finally stood up and put her down on the floor. "Yes, dear." He parroted back to her with a slight bow at the waist.

"If you want to just pack for the week, I can bring you back here this weekend, and we can pack up the rest of your stuff."

She pulled a suitcase out of the closet. "I travel pretty light. I buy clothes as I need to for whatever area I'm in if the weather starts changing, and I donate my old stuff to charity. And I only get furnished places."

He sat on the bed and watched her as she moved around the room between the small dresser and closet. "Did you ever work in the places you stopped?"

She hummed in her throat, "Sometimes. If I was in an area where there was more than one wolf pack, I would stick around longer, wait for that, I don't know, tickle of awareness that I'd found my mate? So I picked up temp jobs."

"So what did you do for money, if you didn't really work?"

"My parents provide for me. They're thrilled to get to stop the gravy train once we're official." She gave him a wink, and he grinned.

"When can that be?"

"When can what be?" She paused in the doorway of the bathroom and looked at him.

"When can we be official?" *Aw, sweetheart.*

"Well, my mom said that we can visit the pack in the spring and make plans then. And," she showed him her bare fingers, "something's missing from this hand anyway."

He looked so happy just then, as if he'd been given a gift he wanted more than anything else in his life. She had already packed up her things after showering earlier, pretty sure he was going to insist she come home with him. It hadn't missed her notice this morning that his wolf was giving him a hard time about leaving. She grabbed her makeup and girlie products and put them in the front pocket of the suitcase.

"Did you want to go anywhere this week or just stay in?" she asked, folding a sweater into the suitcase.

His brow furrowed slightly, and he frowned. She moved to him and nudged his legs apart with her knees and cupped his face. "You can tell me anything, Linus. I won't make fun of you or give you grief for anything you think or feel. Right here," she motioned to the space between them, "is safe for both of us. It's supposed to be that way."

Emotions flickered through his eyes so fast she couldn't get a read on any of them until the end when he looked relieved. His hands kneaded her waist and he looked into her eyes, "I don't want to share you. I'm afraid you'll think I'm ashamed of you or something, but I'm not. When the guys showed up yesterday and they were close to where you were in the bedroom, I could barely keep hold of my beast."

She ran her thumbs along his cheeks, "Okay. So we'll stay in. I have to warn you, though, with this moving in thing: I will flip out if you leave the toilet seat up."

He chuckled, but it sounded forced. At her prompting, he said, "You really want to be with me, even after everything I told you about my past?"

She moved closer and hugged him, pressing his cheek against her shoulder. "I spent fifteen months without a home. I teetered between being pissed off at the length of the journey and being terrified of leaving a place too soon or staying too long. There's nothing easy about my life up to this point. I would have given anything to know you years ago, but I love the man you are now. So, however you came to be who you are, I'm good with it. The more time we spend together, the stronger our bond will grow, and then you'll lose those doubts. I couldn't have picked a better man for myself than you."

His voice was thick with emotion, and he hugged her tighter, burying his face in her neck. "I'm just afraid you're going to be disappointed in me."

"Not possible."

She kissed the top of his head and let him have the few minutes he needed to collect himself. She didn't mind hugging him one bit. Ask her about her fantasies and she would say more often than not that they weren't sexual, but about finding the man she was going to be able to love forever.

"You calm my wolf." He said, kissing her neck.

He pulled back enough to let her see he was over all that emotion. "That's just one of my charms."

He let her go so she could finish packing. "I didn't tell anyone in my pack about you. I mean, they knew you were in the house and that you're human, but I guess you're not entirely human, though. But you're not wolf, and that's what they'd care about."

"No, I'm not entirely human, but other than being made for you and what our children will become, there isn't anything different about me."

He shook his head with an awed smile. "I can't imagine having a son that would be more powerful than me. It's amazing to think about."

"Or you could be like my dad and have three alpha-powerful sons. And my mother has six brothers that are all alphas."

"Are they in the states?"

"Two of them are, out west. My parents wanted me to go out there right away, because they would trust my uncles to keep an eye on me, but I wanted a more methodical search. At least until I started going buggy looking for you. Then it was just me wandering aimlessly and feeling kinda hopeless." She shrugged. "My other uncles are in Europe."

"Do you think your parents will like me?" He fidgeted uncomfortably.

"Of course they will. You're my mate. You're perfect for me. The only reason they wouldn't like you is if I'd tried to force a mating before I found my mate."

He frowned, and she groaned inwardly. She hadn't meant to insult him.

"Linus, I'm sorry."

He cut her off. "No, don't be sorry." He stood slowly and moved around the bed to her. Taking her hands in his, he looked down at her for a few moments and then said, "I'd always worried about telling my future wife about my past, but you just forgive all of that, don't you?"

"Your past makes you who you are right now, and I wouldn't change anything about you."

"I can't believe that you're in my life, Karly. I don't ever want to let you go."

He hugged her close, pulling her against him tightly. "You don't ever have to worry about that," She said into his chest and hugged him back.

He carried her box and both of the suitcases down to his truck, and then he came back for her, carrying her across the hall so she could tell Mrs. Beckinson that she was moving out. It was completely unnecessary for him to carry her, but he insisted and she indulged him. Mrs. B. smiled at Linus as he held Karly in his arms and said, "So you're the young man who saved the best neighbor I ever had?"

"Yes'm." He grinned, and it made his eyes light up.

"You'll visit, dear?"

"Of course, Mrs. B.," she promised, squeezing her hand.

"I'll make sure of it," Linus added and they said goodbye as he carried her all the way out to his truck and set her in the passenger seat. When he sat down in the driver's seat and shut his own door, he said, "Say goodbye to your wandering days, woman; you're all mine now." He gave her a wicked grin and put the truck into gear. What a sweet threat!

Although completely unnecessary, he carried her into the house and seemed to really enjoy it. While he brought in her things, she perused the pantry, thinking about breakfast. He came up behind her, sliding his hands around her waist and growling softly in her ear. "I think I said you weren't going to get any sleep tonight. Did you think I meant you should wait in the kitchen?"

She laughed and ran her hands on his upper arms, "I was planning breakfast."

"Ah. Well, you'll still be up at dawn, so I wouldn't worry about it at the moment."

She spun in his arms and ran her fingers across his jaw. "Won't you be exhausted tomorrow?"

He shrugged, "Karly, there isn't any place else I'd rather be than here with you. If I have to be a little tired for work, then I'm willing to risk it to spend as much time with you as possible." He pursed his lips with a frown. "Are you, do you need space or something? Am I being too clingy?"

She gave him her own version of a growl, and his eyes went wide. She made sure he was looking into her eyes when she said, "I don't want space, you're not too clingy, and I will throttle whoever put those thoughts in your head. You can't compare me to anyone you've ever known, Linus, because I'm unique. Not because I'm awesome or arrogant, but because I'm made just for you. You feel it, don't you? That I belong to you?"

"Yes." His eyes were still wary, but it was fading fast.

"It's because I do. Now, are you going to do something with this or should we just go to bed?" She slid her hand down to cup his erection through his pants and dug her fingertips into the fabric.

"Oh, yeah, we're definitely going to bed."

He scooped her up in his arms and carried her quickly to the bed, following her down to the mattress and pressing his length against her.

Grinding his hips into hers he said, "Are you wearing panties?"

Giving him something of an indignant look, she said, "As if I'm the sort of girl who wouldn't wear panties to dinner."

One hand slid down her side very slowly, edging towards the hem of the short dress. She wondered if he was just guessing. "Somehow I don't believe that innocent look, my sweet angel."

"What?"

His fingers moved slowly upwards and between her legs, which were trapped between his. "I'm thinking I'll just have to check for myself."

She let out a breathless laugh as his fingers edged further up her thighs, and he shifted enough to make it easier to reach the apex of her thighs. His fingers brushed against her bare body, and he grinned. "I love how you think, sweetheart. And can I just say that anytime you don't want to wear panties, I'm totally okay with it."

He kissed her and moved his fingers against her, sliding off the lower part of her body as he sat up. He peeled the dress down slowly, as if they had eternity to make love and not just a handful of hours that night, and kissed and caressed each inch of her flesh that was bared.

She had never been touched quite as thoroughly or intimately as Linus did, and maybe it was supposed to be that way. Maybe the one man that you spend the rest of your life with was the one that was meant to unlock all your secrets. Not just your heart but your body, too.

Seemingly intent on making her melt from the inside, he held her down by her thighs and went to town on the center of her body, until she couldn't do anything but make small mewling noises while she waited for the next plateau of pleasure to sweep over her. Drawing her through a third orgasm, her back bowed off the bed, and it was only his hands on her that kept her in place as she thrashed and writhed under him, begging, "Linus, please, please!"

The heat and pressure of his mouth stopped suddenly, and lifted so that air cooled her overheated flesh. Then she felt his lips, slick with her heat, kissing up the center of her body. His cock nudged her, and he dropped his face to the crux of her neck as he drove himself inside. His groan morphed into a low, long growl, the sound sliding down her spine like an intimate caress. The image in her mind flashed to fangs and claws, and the scent of him deepened, like fall and earth and furred bodies tangled together for warmth and affection. Linus smelled like home. She was finally home.

# CHAPTER SEVEN

The next few days passed both very fast and very slow. Linus marveled at how time was like that. When he was with Karly, the minute hand on the clock seemed possessed, whirling past twelve with lightning speed. It would be five o'clock in the evening and he'd pull her into his arms in the house, and then the alarm was ringing at 6:30 a.m. and he'd have to get ready to leave. But during work, time nearly stopped dead. All an illusion, of course, he knew that time was moving the same no matter what; it was just the feeling of it. As soon as he sat in his truck in the morning, he wanted to go back to her. One more kiss. One more touch. One more of her killer smiles.

When he came home from work Tuesday, she'd unpacked her things and completely reorganized the closet in the master bedroom. He'd told her to make herself at home because it was her home now, and she did. He remembered with a shudder that one woman he'd dated after Brenda had tried to leave a toothbrush in his bathroom after their second date, and he'd gotten a little nuts about that. Probably because he didn't want Brenda to think he'd moved on when he was still so hung up on her. But now, he wanted Karly's imprint on everything in the house.

Wednesday, he'd been surprised that she wasn't in the kitchen when he got home from work, and then his sensitive ears picked up what sounded like sex coming from the bedroom. He raced back, throwing the door open with a growl lodged in his throat. Yes, there were sex sounds in the bedroom, but it was from his porn stash. Karly was splayed out in all her nude glory in the center of the bed, a wicked grin on her face and her fingers between her legs. He recognized the DVD, "Dances with Pussy," and he would have blushed and tried to explain his large collection, except he was frozen to the sight of her touching herself.

"I decided to get started on my own," she purred, her fingers soaked with her sweet juices. He was completely absorbed by the sight in front of him. Except for porn, he'd never seen a woman pleasure herself before, and Karly was incredible. Her body was flushed, her mouth was parted as her teeth grazed the lower swell of her lip, and one hand held her pussy spread wide for his viewing pleasure while the other drove fingers into her depths and swirled the wet heat around her clit.

He smelled the change in her body as she drew closer and closer to climax, and he watched her body grow more tense until she cried out his name when she came. He couldn't have been more turned on by the sight and sound of her. His name. She fucking said his name when she touched herself. He slammed his hand against the off button on the side of the television mounted on the wall above the dresser and stalked to her.

He stripped and looked down at her as she lay sprawled on the bed, breathing hard and shivering. "You're amazing, angel," he said, staring at her pussy that dripped with heat and beckoned him. But it wasn't just her body, it was her eyes, the searing dark brown that seemed bottomless, and the truth he could see in the depths. She might have put on porn, but she'd been thinking about him the whole time. He could see that.

After they made love and he curled her against his side, he said, "Tell me how I got so lucky, Karly."

She kissed his shoulder and sat up, leaning over him. "What do you mean?"

He shrugged. "I'm not anything special. I don't know why you'd pick me as a mate. I don't know what I did to deserve you."

Once more he could see that she didn't like his insinuation that he wasn't worth anything. It was hard to get over a couple dozen years or so of feeling like shit after a few days. His unhappy childhood, the brutal treatment from his father...it was difficult for him to think of himself as a man deserving of such a wonderful woman like her.

And then she suddenly looked hurt. She looked like he'd just punched her in the gut or ran over her puppy with his truck. He sat up and hugged her. "I'm sorry, Karly. I didn't mean to hurt your feelings. I know you didn't pick me out of a lineup, and I know that your powers aren't wrong, I just can't help feeling like you're a dream and I'm going to wake up and be even more miserable than I was. Or that you'll wake up some day and regret being tied to a small-town mechanic with a high school education."

Just as quickly as the hurt had appeared, it dissolved, and she smiled gently and kissed the inside of his palm, using it to cup her cheek. "One of these days, you're not going to doubt my affection for you. My power brought me to you. It didn't make me fall in love with you. That's all me."

She drew him into the circle of her arms, and they held each other until they were both comforted and content. After another of her wonderful meals, they made love in front of the fire on a mound of pillows and fell asleep tangled together as the fire died down.

"Grandma, I wanted to get your ring from you." He shut himself up in the back empty office at the garage and used his cell at lunch on Thursday.

"No."

His heart stopped for a second. "What?"

"I want to meet her first, so you can bring her over for dinner on Friday."

He got a little angry. "I'm going to marry her regardless, Grandma."

She laughed. "Of course you are. It's not about us approving of her; we just want to meet her. And it's exciting for me anyway, Linus, I've never met an Angel. I've always wanted to."

His heart started up again, and his anger vanished. "You won't show her any of my baby pictures will you?"

She laughed and said, "Maybe not me, but your mom might."

"Okay. What time?"

"Let's say seven, so you can have time to get cleaned up after work. And I'll keep mum about the ring. I'm so glad you're asking for it. My mother would be thrilled."

As Linus hung up and went to eat his lunch in the break room, he thought about the ring. It wasn't fancy, but it was special. It had been in his family for generations, carefully passed from one to the next. He'd never been inclined to give it to Brenda. He was pretty sure that if he'd asked his grandmother for it then that she would have meant it when she said no. No one had understood why he married her, and he'd given up trying to explain himself. This was something he could do that was just for Karly. He could honestly say he'd never given anyone else the family ring. He could give her this one thing that was untainted by his past.

"Who the hell is making you all these amazing lunches?" Bo asked, leaning over from his own seat and making eyes at the spread in front of him. Compared to Bo's fast food, Linus was dining on five-star quality food. Today she'd packed from-scratch mac and cheese, two barbecue chicken sandwiches with a sauce she made herself, a plastic container of steamed veggies with cheese sauce, and a dozen peanut butter cookies. He swore she was getting up in the middle of the night to cook for him. He had no idea how she did it all.

He smiled at Bo and picked up a sandwich. He savored the bite of perfectly tender chicken and tangy, sweet sauce and swallowed. "The girl that was in my bedroom on Sunday morning," he lowered his voice even though they were currently the only ones in the break room. "She's my truemate. She's the one that has been cooking for me."

Bo gave him a critical look. "Is this the human that Jason was giving you a hard time about?"

He nodded.

Bo was very quiet, so he went back to eating. With every bite, it was like he could feel his connection to Karly growing, as if he could taste her love for him in the food she prepared. He couldn't wait to mark her. His plan was to get the ring on Friday and then take her out to dinner somewhere very nice on Saturday to propose, then marking her at home later. The thought of her teeth sinking into his flesh, too, as she returned the marks to him, made his heart thud in his chest.

"What's that like?" Bo asked quietly and startled him from his musings and erotic thoughts of the sweetheart back home.

"What's what like?"

"Finding your truemate?"

He finished the last bite of the second sandwich and took a long drink of iced tea from a thermos. It was peach this time. She'd added the juice from a can of sliced peaches after she made a crumble the night before. Clever little angel.

He couldn't stop his smile. "It's amazing. I don't even know if that's a strong enough word." He told him about finding her near death in the snow by the creek and how he'd felt instantly connected to her but didn't realize what it was until they were together the first time. He skipped the part about her being his supernaturally perfect mate, because he wasn't sure that Bo would understand and he didn't want rumors flying around about her.

"So I asked her to move in with me, and she packed up Monday night." Ah, could the mac and cheese be any better? Damn she was a great cook.

"Just like that?"

He shrugged. "I couldn't stand to know she wasn't with me. If I'd had to leave her there Monday night, too, I think I would have camped out on her doorstep all night just to make sure she was safe."

Bo went quiet again and turned back to his greasy burger and fries. Linus dove into the veggies and finished off the pasta before turning his attention to the cookies. How she knew exactly the amount of food he could eat, he wasn't sure, but it was clearly from practice. He always had plenty to eat with no leftovers. While he chewed on the cookies, he looked at Bo who didn't look happy. Bo had problems, but he wasn't the chatty sort. Although they had grown up together, Bo was a year older than he and Jason. He had been struck by a car when he was fourteen, and the damage to one leg was very severe. If he'd been hit after he was sixteen and had the ability to shift, he would have healed most of the damage, but even the change hadn't helped him. He walked with a limp, and he always wore jeans, even in the hottest part of the summer. He'd never had a serious relationship. Bo was one of those silent types that you could trust at your back, but you could never be quite sure what he was thinking.

Linus gave Bo his last cookie. He could be generous, since he'd eaten two dozen last night, licked the bowl, and then just ate eleven. "There's someone for everyone, Bo. Human, wolf, or other. We're made to have mates." He put his things back into the cooler and stood up.

Bo looked up at him with eyes a shade of pain that made Linus suck in a quick breath. "Do you really believe that?"

He swallowed the desire to ask him what was wrong and instead gave him a sincere smile drawn from his own truth, "I really do."

Karly was bent over the counter and writing something furiously when he came into the house after work. His hands slid over the soft curves of her ass through the fabric of her jeans and squeezed. "I love your ass, Karly. Did I mention that?"

She wiggled her hips and tossed her hair over her shoulder as she looked at him, "You might have mentioned it when you were spanking me for watching one of your naughty movies without you."

He growled a laugh and pulled her into his already throbbing erection with his hands on her hips. "I don't mind you watching, I just don't want to miss the whole show next time."

He leaned over her back and hugged her, kissing her neck and cheek. "I missed you, angel."

Dropping the pen, she reached her hands back and clutched at him, "I missed you, too."

He opened his eyes and dropped them to the page she'd torn out of a notebook. It looked like a grocery list. "Do you want me to take you shopping tonight?"

"That would be great." She tried to turn to face him, but he held her still and she immediately relaxed. He reached for the button of her jeans, and she tipped her face up to kiss him. The zipper fell slowly, that low sound of the metal teeth parting, and he slid his tongue into her mouth and tasted whatever she was making for dinner and had been tasting before he got home. Red meat and wine. Delicious.

He found the edge of her panties, tiny little things that they always were, and she moaned and pulled back, "If we play, then dinner will be cold, and I'm nearly out of things to cook for us."

"Just you, angel. Let me touch you."

Her head dropped back to his shoulder and tilted enough so he could kiss her neck, and he slid his hand to her pussy underneath her panties and found her wet and hot. She had not denied him yet. No matter what he asked, she went willingly. She teased and tormented him, but the way she let him play with her made him want to do it more and more.

She tugged her jeans down her hips for him, and he rewarded her by sinking two fingers inside her and caressing her clit with the palm of his hand. He sucked on her neck, hard enough to bruise, and her pussy clenched his fingers. He slid his hand around to her throat and splayed his fingers across the length of her neck to hold her firmly in place while he bruised her throat with his mouth and fucked her with his fingers. His fingers pounded into her until he wrenched a scream of pleasure from her lips and her nails dug into his arms where she held onto him for dear life.

Her climax seeped over his fingers as her body clenched him again and again in little waves, and she let out a sobbing sigh. Her knees gave out, and she leaned heavily into the counter. He licked the dark purple bruise on her neck and nuzzled under her ear. Pulling his hand free, he showed her the glistening wetness, and she shivered. "I love what you let me do to you, angel," he said with a rough voice.

She sniffled and turned her face to him, and he caught sight of a tear on her cheek. He kissed it away. When she was really pleasured, taken right to that highest point he could take her, tears would stream down her face. It had freaked him out the first time, worried he'd hurt her, but now he knew what it meant. She was just that happy.

"Now, pull up your jeans like a good girl, and let's eat dinner and go shopping," he gave her ass a light smack.

"We could have a quickie."

He licked one of his fingers. Exquisite. "Nah. I'd rather wait and take my time. Why would I want to be fast with you, sweetheart?"

She tugged up her jeans and turned around, leaning against the counter. Her eyes were bright and happy, and a wicked little smile played across her mouth. "You weren't planning on getting any sleep tonight, were you?"

"Nah." He murmured.

"Good thing."

She watched him while he licked his fingers clean of the intoxicating taste of her come. Fuck, he loved her watching him.

Dinner was amazing. Something she called Beef Bourguignon with a red wine sauce. He didn't even realize he had red wine in the house, but she'd found it in the back of one of the kitchen cabinets. The last of the canned potatoes were roasted with baby carrots and little onions in the gravy, and she made a chocolate pie for dessert.

While he drove her to the grocery in town, he said, "So we've been invited to dinner on Friday at my grandma's house. My grandpa will be there, and my mom, too."

She was leaning across the seat with her head on his shoulder and hugging his arm. "They want to meet me?"

"Of course."

"And they know about what I am? What we are together?"

"Yeah. My grandma is the one that recognized the tattoo."

"My tattoo?" She looked up at him, and he glanced down at her.

"Um, Monday at lunch when I was over at her house fixing her sink, she asked me to wait while she got something for me. I was doodling on the newspaper and it was your tattoo. She asked who I knew that was an

Angel."

"You drew my tattoo from memory?"

"Memory? Hell, Karly, I spent a long time kissing and licking that mark over the weekend. It's burned into my brain."

She laughed and leaned up far enough to kiss him on the cheek. "You're such a sweetheart. How'd I get so lucky?"

Well, they weren't going to argue about who was luckiest in their relationship. He was clearly the winner.

She offered to help pay for the groceries. He tried not to let his pride get wounded. He truly didn't think she asked because she didn't think he could afford it but because she was just polite and wanted to share in their responsibilities. She only offered once, and he turned her down with a kiss and a thanks-but-no-thanks, so she let it go. She wanted to shop for a week's worth of groceries. "But not Friday of course, and I'd like to take you out to dinner on Saturday, if you're interested," he said.

He walked next to her while she pushed the cart through the first aisle that was dairy products. Even though she had a list, she didn't even check it. It seemed to be memorized. "Sure," she smiled and flashed him her dimple.

They talked about food in the grocery. What else was there to talk about? He found out her favorite meal was chicken parmesan, but she also liked a good grilled steak, rare of course, and her favorite dessert was strawberries with chocolate sauce. She loved her parents and had a pretty charmed life, even for growing up in a strict old-school wolf pack. She had a few nieces and nephews courtesy of her three alpha werewolf brothers, and had last seen her parents at Christmas.

After he unloaded the groceries, he waited until she had the cold things put away and then chased her back into the bedroom, "I've waited long enough, Karly."

* * * * * * *

"You look dead beat, man," Michael mused from where he leaned casually against the workbench. "Is your new girl keeping you up all night?"

Linus looked up at him from where he was kneeling next to the bike he was determined to finish today. "Yeah."

"What's her name?"

"Karly."

He hummed in his throat. "She's human, right?"

"Yep." Eventually it would come out, but it would be on their terms and no one else's. He could guess that Bo had talked to Jason. Linus had expected as much.

"You didn't learn your lesson the first time?" Michael sniffed derisively. A few weeks ago, he would have throttled Michael for the insult. Now, though, he could see it came from a dark place. Michael wasn't happy.

"No, actually, I learned my lesson well. Karly's my mate. My truemate. If she needed my heart to live, I'd cut it from my chest myself. That's never happened to me before. I've never felt that way about anyone."

Michael's eyes shadowed darkly. "Must be nice," he muttered as he walked away and back to his own work.

* * * * * * *

The house smelled like fruit when he got home, and he found his little sweetheart putting a still warm-from-the-oven dessert into a plastic container. She smiled as he kissed her cheek, "It's an apricot braid. For your family."

He marveled at her sweetness again. He showered and shaved quickly, and when he went into the closet, he found his one pair of dress slacks pressed and hanging neatly. He'd planned to wear jeans tonight and try to iron them for tomorrow. He barked for Karly.

"Yeah, sweetie?" She walked into the bedroom a few moments later.

He was going to tell her that she shouldn't do his laundry. That he didn't want her to feel obligated or that he expected her to act like some 1950s housewife, but the moment he saw her eyes, he knew it wasn't about any of that for her. She just flat-out wanted to take care of him, and for her, that meant this exact thing. He hung the slacks back up and held his arms out for her. She crossed the distance quickly and sighed into his chest. "Thank you, love."

"What for?"

"For everything that you do for me. You make me feel very loved. Do I make you feel that way, too?"

Her brown eyes were warm and kind, "Most definitely."

There was something that tickled at the back of his mind while he held her against him and rocked back and forth quietly. An old saying, maybe that he'd heard as a child. That the husband was the warrior that protected the home and the wife was the warrior that protected his heart. But she wasn't just protecting his heart; she was the living, breathing epitome of it.

As he expected, his family loved her. They peppered her with questions about her family's pack, her upbringing as an angel, and her journey to find him. He listened with pride as she described her search for him, as if he were the most important man in the universe for her. And he guessed that he was. When they got ready to leave, his grandmother slipped an envelope into his jacket pocket, and he smiled in thanks to her.

Saturday morning they went back to her apartment and finished gathering her things. Her clothes and her Angel books were all at the house, but her art supplies and camera equipment that she lugged from city to city were waiting to find a place in the house. He couldn't wait to look through her albums. She spoke with such an excited gleam in her eyes when she talked about photography and art. He wanted the walls in the house full of her pictures.

On the way to her tiny apartment, they stopped at a dog breeder she had apparently contacted during the week, and she picked out a little female rat terrier puppy. He managed to find the frozen body of the original dog in the creek at her request. She'd bundled it carefully in a cardboard box, and they had given the puppy and the dead dog to her neighbor, who was going to take it to a pet cemetery. He took the opportunity of the mutual tears of the two women to load up her things, and then he reminded Karly that they had plans and needed to get going.

She followed him home in her fantastic Porsche Boxter. She said it was her father's, and he apparently liked to get a new car every year and donated his old ones to his children. It fit perfectly in the garage after he moved his motorcycle to make room for it. He was itching to drive it, too, and have his arm around her while he did it.

"Now, you said we had plans?" she asked, watching the garage door slide shut.

"Um, naked plans, yep." He laughed and swung her up over his shoulder and carried her back to the bedroom like the caveman he felt like. It was going to be a great weekend.

# CHAPTER EIGHT

He said nice restaurant, and he had grabbed his only pair of dress slacks and one of his two dress shirts, so she took the hint and looked through her dressy things and finally settled on a pretty v-neck sweater dress that she paired with black stiletto heels.

He was looking out the back door when she walked out of the bedroom. The black slacks and dark blue dress shirt looked wonderful, and the tie was black and blue checks. The shirt offset his eyes and made them look darker than they really were – blue jean and not baby blue. Gorgeous, nonetheless.

He folded her in his arms, "You are so beautiful, sweetheart."

"You are as sweet as you are handsome."

She could see he was going to do that arguing thing where he was going to tell her that she was the better part of the relationship, so she silenced him with a kiss.

He drove to a restaurant about twenty minutes away. The ride was quiet and he held her hand on his thigh but he seemed nervous and tense. When he parked in front of the Italian restaurant, he got out of his side and came around to hers and opened the door for her, holding her hand as she hopped down.

They were seated at a small table in the dimly lit restaurant, punctuated with a roaring fireplace and candles on the tables. It was definitely romantic. She played conversation-keeper and asked him about the garage and the bike he had just finished that afternoon, his friends, and pack news. The full moon wasn't for three more weeks.

He told her about his friend Bo who seemed very unhappy and lonely, and the second in the pack, Michael, who was the smartass of their group of friends.

Dinner was wonderful. They shared a tiramisu and talked over coffee, and then he was ready to take them home. He seemed to get more nervous as the evening drew to a close. He asked her to give him a minute in the family room alone, so she went into the bedroom and sat on the bed and waited. He came to get her about ten minutes later and held her hand in his and led her back out. A fire crackled in the fireplace, candles twinkled on every surface, and a blanket had been spread out and large pillows tossed casually around the edges. An open bottle of wine and two glasses were on the end table.

He pulled her to the center of the blanket, and before she could do anything, he dropped down to one knee and her heart stopped beating.

He pulled a ring from his pocket and looked up at her. In the firelight and candlelight, she could see clearly that there was a part of him that worried she would say no. That she might not really believe they were mates.

"Karly, my sweet angel, I love you. I know it's only been a week, but I couldn't imagine my life without you in it. And I want to marry you. I want you to have my last name and make a family with me. I want to spend the rest of my life making you the happiest woman in the world. Will you marry me?"

Tears slid down her cheeks, "Oh, Linus, of course I'll marry you."

He pushed the band onto her finger and stood up slowly, hugging her tightly and kissing her hungrily.

They made love on the pillows on the floor as the fire flickered orange and yellow across their bodies, and when he had caught his breath, he said, “Sweetheart, can I mark you?”

She lifted her head from his chest where she had been listening to his heart pound and said, “Of course.”

“Are you sure?”

She tried not to roll her eyes. “I said I would marry you. Why wouldn’t I also want to wear your marks?”

“I just…wanted to make sure.”

She rolled off him and flipped her hair off her neck, stretching out on her side. “I’m positive. Mark me, Linus, make me yours in truth.”

She could smell his body change. He smelled great all the time, all male and warmth and the cologne he liked, but as he shifted slightly so his fangs elongated, she caught the scent of his wolf, like deep earth in the fall. Comforting.

“I love you, Karly. My sweet Angel Mate.” He said with a rough voice as his breath skirted over her neck. Tilting her head to get the angle he wanted, he sank his fangs onto either side of her spine, and her body lit up. It hurt, but not worse than anything else she’d ever been through, and the emotions that came with it overpowered the pain as it slid into pleasure.

She reached for his hand that was resting on her hip and moved it between her legs, and his groan shifted to a growl that slid down her spine and lodged there. His fangs receded as his fingers slid into her pussy, and he licked the marks and the blood that seeped from them and drove her to an orgasm. They made love again, and she rode him this time.

Their emotions tangled together, and she could feel his utter awe at the situation and the love that filled the whole center of his being. As another orgasm crested through her, she did what she knew he wanted but would never ask. She jerked him up by his shoulders and sank her teeth into his neck. He roared as he came, holding her so tight she could scarcely catch a breath as her teeth cut through his skin and his blood seeped into her mouth. The very raw power of his blood, the final part of their bond as mates, coursed through her, and she felt as primal as she ever had. She licked across the marks as she held him tightly in place with her hands fisted in his hair. Unlike a human's marks on a wolf's flesh, hers would scar just like his would, but only this time when her blood was in his veins and his in hers.

She touched the marks with her fingertips, "These will be here forever, Linus."

He loosened his grip with a shaky breath and looked surprised, "Really? I'll get to keep them?"

She smiled softly and kissed his cheek, "Of course. I'm a supernatural being. And these were the right circumstances. You marked me and took my blood into your body, and with your blood in me, it gave me the ability to make these marks permanent. I tried to keep them towards the back of your neck. And they're not as neat as if I had real fangs." She paused, "Was that okay? I should have asked."

He slid his hands up her sweaty arms and cupped her face, "Sweetheart, I'm so glad. I wasn't sure you would want to mark me every few days for the rest of our lives." He smiled genuinely.

He seemed to suddenly remember that he had wine for them, so they toasted their future together. After they both went to the bathroom to check out their new marks, they settled back together in front of the fire, and she got a chance to look at the ring for the first time. It was a simple band of woven white gold.

He fingered it and said, "I want to get you one from me, too, sweetheart, but this is my family's band, and I needed you to have it. You're the only one I have ever wanted to give it to. I need you to know that." He looked at her, and a very sad little boy was peeking through his eyes. She'd caught glimpses of this part of him. Whether it was the childhood he didn't want to talk about or the ex-wife that had caused him so much grief, there was a part of this man that expected to be hurt. That steeled himself for it.

"I love it. And I love you, Linus. I truly do."

They made love again, and although they fell asleep on the pillows in front of the fireplace, she woke up in his arms in bed and couldn't have been happier.

The following week passed quickly. Her mom shipped two boxes of her things she'd left at home, mostly her shoe collection, and she spent her days cooking and cleaning and taking care of her future husband. It was all very "Leave It To Beaver," but she loved it. It's what she'd always wanted. She certainly wasn't one of those girls who thought that it was an insult to take care of her man. When he would call at lunchtime to thank her for whatever she'd put together for him, she could just hear the walls around his heart cracking; as if every time he called there was a worry at the back of his mind that she might not be there this time and he was relieved that she was. And the way he called her name at night when he got home from work...like she might have changed her mind and taken off. Time was what would help him to realize she wasn't going anywhere, and that she would definitely give him.

He wanted to see her photography albums, so they spent one evening going through them. She had several professional cameras and loved to take nature pictures. One particularly stunning picture of a solid charcoal gray wolf standing in a snow laden forest stopped him. "This is incredible." He said quietly.

"It's my favorite. That's my dad."

"No kidding?"

"My mom wanted a picture of him in his shift for her birthday. He told me if I could find him, I could take his picture, and he shifted and took off. I'm a pretty good tracker, but it took me all day to catch up to him and he wasn't really trying that hard not to be found, too. Would you let me take your picture some day?"

"Yeah?"

"Sure. If I have a picture of you, I could do an oil painting from it. I think it would be smashing over the fireplace."

"I would love it."

Although he hadn't seemed to want her to go out on her own in town, when she insisted that she wanted to go to the grocery while he was at work, plus to get out of the house a little, he left her cash on the counter before he left that morning. She tooled around the small town before she went to the only grocery. She found the bar called Jake's that was only open on Friday and Saturday nights, the bank, the deli, and the grocery, and then Pete's Garage where Linus worked. She was extremely tempted to drop in under the pretense of getting gas, but she wasn't sure he could handle it. They'd just marked each other, and some wolves got territorial with their mates for the first few weeks. If her presence caused him to attack his friends, she would feel terrible.

He suggested they could go to the bar on Saturday to have a drink and so she could meet his alpha and some of the pack, but only if she promised to let him be all possessive and nuts, which she happily agreed to. She was curious about the pack that he was part of that was so modern that they had abandoned many of the old ways that she'd grown up with.

"Um, no." he said Saturday night, leaning against the doorway of the closet and folding his arms in a final sort of way.

"No, what?" She looked at him in confusion as she adjusted her favorite Ed Hardy leather belt on her low rider leather pants.

"No on the top."

She looked down at herself. The top was plain black stretchy material that had one long sleeve and no sleeve on the other side, cutting across from the one shoulder down under the arm, and leaving the other shoulder and arm bare. It was just the right length to hit above her belly button.

"You don't like it?"

"I like it very much, Karly, but so will every other man in the bar. So, no."

She narrowed her eyes at him and put her hands on her hips. "I'm not going to dress like a nun in front of your friends forever."

"Not a nun, just less like you're advertising things that aren't for sale."

"I wasn't aware I was dressed like a billboard," she said dryly.

"Sweetheart, please? I want to introduce you to my friends, but I, hell, maybe this isn't a good idea." He sighed and went from looking like he wasn't going to take no for an answer about her clothes to looking defeated. She hated that look. It was as if he thought his feelings had no value.

She gave him a shove towards the bed. "Alright, give me a minute to pick out something less-billboardy."

He breathed a sigh of relief. She stripped off the top and flipped through her things. "Can I keep the pants on?"

"Depends. Are you wearing panties?"

She peeked her head out of the closet. "A thong. I don't do panty lines in leather; it's like a cardinal girl rule."

He frowned in thought, "I guess you can keep them on."

She chuckled to herself as she turned back around and finally made a choice that she thought he'd appreciate. She had given most of her summer things to charity before she bought clothes for fall, but she kept a few things she liked. One of them was a black tank. It had a shelf bra in it and was form fitting, extra material from the sides gathered in a knot in the front. She pulled one of his casual button down shirts from the hanger, black of course, and slid it on. After she put on her black ankle boots, she walked out as she rolled up the sleeves.

"Wait, I'm not done." She walked into the bathroom and pulled her hair up into a high ponytail. If someone looked at her neck, they'd see his marks. Four white dots, two thicker than the others, on either side of her spine.

"Better?" she asked, when she came out of the bathroom.

He stood up and pulled her into his arms. She let out a yelp and laughed as he kissed and hugged her close. "Much. You're covered, and you smell like me even more with the shirt."

"Linus, you have to know that even if someone was stupid enough to approach me that there isn't anyone else that I want to touch me for the rest of my life but you."

"Well," he smoothed his fingers to where the marks were, "they wouldn't just be stupid they'd be hospitalized very shortly after."

"And?"

He blinked. "And what?"

"And, you don't want to touch anyone else for the rest of your life either."

He snorted and rolled his eyes, "Hell, Karly, I don't want to even look at another woman for the rest of my life, let alone touch one. But women don't look at me the way that men will look at you."

It was her turn to snort. "You're overestimating my appeal."

He got that pissed look in his eyes when he thought she was undervaluing herself. "Um, not even close. If we make it through tonight without me punching my friends then we'll be doing great."

She went up on her toes and nipped at his jaw, and he squeezed her lower back with both hands and sighed, the stress of whatever situation he was imaging might happen at the bar sliding away from him. At least for now.

As they pulled into the parking lot of Jake's Bar, it didn't look like anything special to her. The pack had their own entrance at the back of the bar so they didn't have to stand in line out front, which in the winter was a very good thing. The bar had only been open on the weekends for the last two weekends, and they were waiting for feelers that the alpha had put out to other packs in surrounding states for wolves that would want to jump ship and join up with them and run the bar. So far that hadn't panned out.

Linus pulled her into his arms and began to carry her across the parking lot. "Linus, I can walk."

"I know, angel, but the parking lot is icy and it's cold as hell and your legs are short so I can carry you faster than you can walk."

She huffed, "My legs are perfectly sized for my body. We can't all be giants."

He stopped walking and looked down at her, "You're right. Your legs are the perfect size to wrap around my waist when we're making love. But I won't let you walk over ice. I'm not an asshole. It's not safe."

She let it drop because he had this way of arguing about her safety, and she wondered if he would prefer she was covered in bubble wrap. And sometimes she thought that he wondered what would have happened if she had died out in the snow. It seemed like whenever that thought crossed his mind, he got a little over protective. She truly didn't mind; she just enjoyed giving him a hard time.

When the door opened, they were in a dark, wood paneled hallway. Music was muffled through the walls but loud enough she was sure it was going to burst her ear drums, and she was totally right. When he put her down and opened the door into the bar for her, she was nearly bowled over by the music. He took her hand firmly in his after a quick scan of the tables and pulled her behind him towards the right side of the very busy bar.

He didn't give her much slack, holding her hand very close to him as he maneuvered them through the throng of tables, around the small dance area, and to the line of u-shaped booths along the wall. She felt him grow nervous and squeezed his hand for reassurance.

He stopped at a booth in the middle. There were four people in it. Two dark blonde males, one brunette female, and a black haired male.

"Linus," the male in the center of the booth said, sliding his arm around the brunette female possessively. He had dark blond hair, a goatee, and serious blue eyes.

"Jason." Linus took a slow breath and said, "This is Karly. Karly, this is our alpha Jason, his mate Cadence, Michael our second, and Bo our third."

Everyone at the table stared at her in silence. Not unfriendly but not exactly welcoming either. They stood in silent limbo for several moments, and then Cadence elbowed Jason and he shook his head as if clearing thoughts from it. "Nice to meet you Karly. You can join us if you'd like."

Everyone shifted, and Linus put her inside next to Cadence and sat on the end. He put his arm around her and held her hand with his other hand under the table.

Bo stood up, "Would you guys like a beer or something? We don't have table service right now."

Linus said, "Just a couple sodas, Bo, that would be great."

Bo nodded and walked off as Michael grunted in disbelief, "Since when do you drink soda at a bar, Linus?"

Linus bristled, "Since I have someone riding in the truck with me, and I don't want to impair my driving ability."

The frowns and stunned looks told her that it wasn't typical for Linus to talk like that or to turn down beer. She wouldn't embarrass him by pointing it out, though. She would offer to drive, but she didn't know the town well enough yet to get them home in the dark and he would most definitely turn her down anyway.

Bo returned a few minutes later with two sodas. At that moment, the DJ who had taken a break started the music going again. Some women walked by, giggling in that way that girls will when they're out with their friends, and she caught Michael looking after them in a longing sort of way. Maybe Bo wasn't the only one that was lonely. Karly thought it was different for wolves. Not all of them were lucky enough to get a real mate; they stayed in their own pack and settled down with someone they loved but not necessarily the right wolf for them. Mates weren't always in the home pack. Looking for a mate, waiting and taking your time – that was how the packs stayed fresh and didn't grow stagnant. If no new wolves went out to find mates and start families, then, eventually the pack imploded on itself from lack of new blood. Teenagers left for greener pastures but not with the pack in mind, and families disappeared to nothing.

Linus was very calm, but she could tell it was partly from holding onto her and also because he was doing a very good job of reining in his emotions. If he was nervous, everyone around them would know, and wolves were really funny about nerves.

A woman with honey-brown colored hair came over to the table, "Hey guys," she turned to Karly, "Hi, I'm Callie."

"Karly, nice to meet you," she said and extracted her hand from Linus' with some difficulty to shake her offered one. Bo scooted over and Callie sat down.

"So are you from around here, Karly?" she asked.

"I'm from West Virginia."

Brows were raised by everyone around the table. Michael said, "Did you come here for work or something?"

"No, I was traveling, trying to figure out where to settle down."

The curious brows shifted slightly toward wary, and she felt Linus get tense. Then he picked up her left hand and put it on the table. Five pairs of eyes caught the ring on her ring finger.

Linus said, "I asked Karly to marry me last weekend. Her father is second in his pack, her mother is human."

Bo and Michael looked dumbfounded. After several quiet moments, Callie broke the silence, "Congratulations, Linus and Karly. I'm so happy for you both." She smiled genuinely, and Cadence and the others gave their congratulations as well.

Linus relaxed slowly after that, slipping into a conversation with Bo about trucks, and she leaned into his side and watched the beads of water gather on the outside of the glass in front of her. She wasn't really thinking about anything in particular, but she wasn't paying attention to the conversation either.

"Karly?" Linus said.

She snapped from her thoughts of nothing and blinked up at him. "Sorry, what?"

He smiled in that understanding way he had, like he thought she couldn't ever do anything wrong and apparently repeated himself, "I just offered to host a pack meeting tomorrow night, around dinnertime, at the house. I wanted to make sure you were okay with that."

She straightened. The chance to cook for the pack was quite an honor, especially for someone so new like her. "Of course, Linus, whatever you want."

Michael grumbled under his breath, and Linus darted a glare at him but looked back at her with adoration in his baby blues, "It will just be the top ranked, so not the whole pack."

Her head spun as she started to plan the meal in her mind, and he looked into her eyes for a little bit longer as if he thought maybe she wasn't okay with them being at the house, but she totally was. She needed to show Linus that she could handle being part of his life because she'd grown up being taught just how to do it. Although their pack was more modern than hers, Linus was her mate and these people were his closest friends. If they were unsure of her because they thought she was human and his ex was a nutcase, then she would just have to prove otherwise. And the greatest proof would be Linus' happiness...and time.

Eventually, everyone at the table relaxed, and although she was only half listening because she was putting recipes together in her head, she did find out that Jason and Cadence had only been married for about two months. They were still getting used to being with someone full time. Karly guessed that spoke to how a person viewed marriage and mating. She'd spent so much time alone, searching for the man that she could wake up to every morning for the rest of her life, that she craved their coming marriage. But some people, perhaps Jason and Cadence, spent a long time alone and enjoyed their solitude. Those were the sorts of couples that fought over which side of the bed they slept on or who controlled the remote. Personally, Karly didn't care what side of the bed she slept on as long as Linus was holding her, and as far as the remote went, she couldn't say how often he'd turned on the TV to watch something and they'd ended up missing it completely.

As time dragged by, she was not only bored stiff with sitting in the booth and not really being included in any conversations but she also had to pee. She patted Linus' hand that had been parked on her shoulder for at least an hour and told him she needed to get up. He walked with her to the bathroom even though she protested she could go on her own, but that possessive look was back in his eyes and she knew he wouldn't want her out of his sight so she dropped it.

"You're being really quiet," he said as they made their way past the throng of tables towards the back where the bathrooms were located.

She didn't want to sound petulant, because in truth she only really cared about talking to him, but it wasn't as if any of his friends were being overly friendly. She wasn't sure she could say anything that wouldn't make him feel bad. "I'm not exactly being included in any conversations."

He stopped abruptly, and she crashed into his shoulder. He looked worried and angry, and he cast his eyes back towards the booth, then he dropped them to hers and slid his thumb across her jaw, hooking his hand behind her neck. "You don't really like this, do you? Sitting in a bar and basically doing nothing."

She shrugged, "It's not really my thing. I'd much rather be home with you or out doing something, not just," she stumbled trying to find the right words, "not just sitting at a table with people that don't trust me not to hurt you."

"I'm really sorry. I should be doing a better job of including you in the conversation. I basically hung you out to dry."

"It's okay, Linus, I promise. Now, I really need to pee, so lead on or get out of the way."

His smile was forced, but he gave it to her anyway, turning and taking her hand in his and leading her to the bathroom. She left him in the hallway and went inside to use the facilities. As she smoothed her hair back and adjusted her top, she wondered what they saw when they looked at her. Another Chew Toy werewolf groupie, looking to bang the big bad? Maybe. Probably. She shuddered at the thought.

When she walked out of the bathroom, the first thing she saw was that Linus looked furious. His face was harsh planes and banked anger, and it was all directed at a tall woman with dark hair, wearing trampy club clothes. All that anger – she had to be his ex. Well, wasn't that just icing on the cake of the evening?

Karly slid her arm around him, and the woman looked down her long nose at Karly with surprise that quickly flickered to hurt and anger when Karly's left hand rested on Linus' stomach and the ring glinted in the light. Linus put his arms around Karly protectively and made motions to turn away from her without a word when the woman sneered, "Aren't you going to introduce me, Linus baby?" The sneer slid into a pout that was all practice. She was clearly used to getting her own way.

A fine tremble went through Linus that Karly recognized as fury. She wasn't too thrilled with the woman calling him "Linus baby," either.

Sucking his teeth in annoyance, he said, "This is my fiancée Karly. Karly, this is Brenda, my ex-wife."

Karly stared at her and only nodded. She was kind of pretty in that angular way that some women could be, prettier from a distance than close up. She couldn't imagine that Linus was attracted to her, but then he'd said that he tried to force things with her, so she may just have been one of the first to express an interest in marriage.

Brenda's eyes narrowed. "Fiancé? My you move fast, Linus. You didn't mention anything about being serious with someone when we talked last."

He practically growled, "I don't see how it's any of your business."

He took a step back, pulling Karly with him, and Brenda made a face that was halfway between annoyed and pissed off. Then something flickered in the depths of her eyes, and Karly was pretty sure that neither of them would like what she said next. "But, Linus, it wasn't too long ago that you were calling me and begging me for sex. I'm just wondering how satisfied you actually are with your little woman there if she's not satisfying you in bed like I can."

Karly had just a heartbeat to step between Linus and Brenda as he took a step forward, his body poised to throttle her. He bumped into Karly's back and froze, and she took over for him because she wasn't emotionally invested and drowning in the situation.

"Whatever you think you're going to accomplish by baiting my fiancé, it won't work. You fucked up with him, which makes you not only a total loser but an idiot to boot. He's mine now, so you can suck on it."

Karly pulled him away from the hallway where Brenda stood boiling in anger. "Do we have to stay?" Karly asked when they were closer to the booth.

"No," he said simply as they got to the booth and put on their coats and said goodbye. When they were on the way home, he said, "I'm really sorry about her. I haven't seen her in a long time; she stopped coming to the bar months ago."

"You don't have to apologize for her behavior; you're not responsible for it."

"This is what I worried about. That I'd have to tell the woman I really love that my past is a fucked up thing."

When the garage door shut behind the truck and the engine was off, he put his head on the steering wheel. "Nothing about tonight went right."

"What did you think would happen? Your pack thinks I'm human. Your ex is jealous and tried to cause a problem for us. I don't really care about any of that. You're fourth in rank to your pack, and you grew up with them. They care about you enough to worry about your choices. When they know what I am and that I'm not going anywhere, then they'll accept me. The only person whose opinion matters to me is you. If you're happy with me, then everyone else can just go to hell."

He turned his head slowly and looked at her. She couldn't get a read on his emotions. "I am happy with you. I have so many regrets. You don't seem to have any at all."

"No, that's not true. I have plenty of regrets. And my biggest regret is not finding you sooner." She pulled him away from the steering wheel and hugged him tightly, kissing his temple and down his cheek to his mouth where she swallowed the whimper of need he made and kissed him.

They barely made it out of the truck with their clothes on, and it was only because the air inside the cab started to chill and she shivered that he opened the door and pulled her out with him, carrying her inside and to the bedroom.

Linus had demons. His childhood, the pack, his first marriage. She had her own demons, too, but she'd had a happy childhood and a strong family foundation and often that went very far in making you the person you were. Plus, she had a supernatural destiny to fulfill in finding her mate and starting the next generation of Angel Mates. However long it took Linus to share everything with her about his childhood, all his past pain and regrets, she would be there for all of it. If she'd learned one thing over the years of watching her parents and the mates within the pack, it was that you didn't get to pick the baggage your mate came with, but once you chose them, then it became your burden as well.

# CHAPTER NINE

Brenda stared at Linus and that little bitch as they left the bar. She had some nerve! And Linus, acting like she'd done something horribly wrong. A few weeks ago, she could have met him in the bar and guaranteed a good fuck, maybe a nice dinner, and some cash to pad her wallet. He wasn't the best lover, but he was eager and he never asked her to reciprocate things like blow jobs, which she absolutely hated.

Being stuck at that loser's house during the blizzard had made her reevaluate her choice in pushing Linus aside, but now...he was engaged? She was new in town, that was for sure, but maybe she was a wolf and that's why he'd jumped onto the marriage wagon so fast again. After all, they'd been apart for three years now, but he always had time for her when she needed something.

And she did need something. A few things. There was something wrong with her car. She was having trouble making rent. Oh yeah, and her biological clock was ticking so loudly it was keeping her up at night. By the time her mother was twenty-seven, she'd had four kids and three husbands and a string of lovers a mile long. When they were married, Linus wanted a baby with her, but she'd stayed on birth control. She wasn't planning to have a child for a long time and was saving it for a bargaining chip when she needed him to do something big for her, like send her on a vacation. But now, that time was here. She wanted to have a baby with a man that would do all the work for her, and that man was Linus.

She returned to the table where her two friends sat discussing the available men in the newly reopened bar. There was a new DJ who came with his own groupies and buddies and several of the guys were good looking. Felicity said, "What's up with the girl with your ex?"

Brenda snorted and twirled the straw in the Seven & Seven. "She's just a fling, don't worry."

Greta laughed, "I don't know what you see in that guy. There are so many other good looking dogs around. Like that Michael. He's so yummy!"

Brenda did think that Michael was good looking, but he also hated her with a passion ever since she and Linus had split. She wasn't about to go down without a fight, though. Linus belonged to her, and she was going to figure out some way to get him back.

An opportunity presented itself later that week when she was in the checkout line at the grocery during her lunch hour and the bitch came in. Brenda waited in her car until she left the store and followed her to her parking spot and wrote down her license plate. She could dig up some dirt on her and maybe give Linus a reason to walk away from her.

"Come on, Greta, I'll do anything if you just look up this license plate for me and tell me about her." Brenda whined, leaning over the desk of the police station where Greta answered the phones.

Greta lowered her voice, "I could get fired for unauthorized access, Bren, no way!"

"I'll do anything, come on!"

Greta's eyes narrowed, and she said, "Give me your black halter dress."

"That's my favorite dress!"

"It's mine or you get nothing," Greta leaned back in her chair, a triumphant smile on her face.

"Fine, fine. It's yours. Now do your thing."

Greta typed in the license plate from West Virginia into the police nationwide database. Taking a glance towards the Chief's office and making sure the door was still shut, she began to write as she spoke.

"Okay, the car is in a man's name, Kamren Nylock, in West Virginia. Let me see if I can run the last name for that county." A few more clicks and some fast typing and she sighed, "There are only two women with the last name of Nylock. One is Sophia and she's forty-seven, and the other is probably who you saw: Karolyn A. Nylock. She's twenty-three. Her home address is West Virginia. Um, oh, this is interesting. She's got a restraining order on some guy named Phoenix Thompson, from her hometown."

Brenda perked up at that tidbit. "A restraining order? Does it say anything about it?"

Greta's finger clicked on the mouse several times, and she said, "There are a handful of police reports for stalking, trespassing, damage to private property, and even...oh, he broke her arm. That's what got the restraining order. He's not allowed within five hundred yards of her. It happened this past fall. Wow, he's not a nice guy at all."

Nope. Not a nice guy at all. But maybe he was the answer to her problems. With a little more coaxing, she got his last known address, thanked Greta for her help, and went home to write a letter.

# CHAPTER TEN

"I think she's great, man. If I didn't say that on Sunday after that incredible dinner, then I definitely feel that way after lunch today," Bo grinned at Linus across the break room table on Friday afternoon. She'd called his cell and told him she needed gas and would he mind if she came to the station. He met her out at the pumps and then she'd asked him to get the boxes out of the trunk. She'd brought lunch for everyone.

The home-style meal was made up of fried chicken, BBQ pulled pork, potato salad, pasta salad, corn bread, and two pans of fudge topped brownies. She only stayed long enough to set all the food up and then kissed him goodbye and left. Damn but he loved her!

Leaning back on two chair legs, Linus wadded up the napkin and rested his hand on his more than stuffed stomach. "I'm glad you like her, Bo. She's special."

Michael threw his napkin at him, "She's a fucking gourmet, and you've got her chained up at your place like it's *Little House on the Prairie*. She should be cooking at Lonestar's. That place would be in the black in a month with her skills manning the stove."

"I do not have her chained up at the house," he bristled, "and I did tell her that she's really talented in the kitchen but she just doesn't think it's anything special. She grew up cooking and that's what she knows."

"When are you going to meet her family?" Bo asked, scraping his plate to catch a last bite of pulled pork.

"End of March when the weather is better. Her dad wants me to go hunting with his pack on the full moon. Her brothers are even planning to come in for our visit."

"Her brothers, the alphas?" Bo asked with wide eyes.

He nodded. Sunday, everything about Karly had come out to the pack. At first, they had just stared blankly at him, and then Jason's father Peter just shook his head in awe after looking through Karly's angel book and said he thought the angel line had all but disappeared in the states. With his acceptance and Karly's re-telling of the legend of the first angel and the first werewolf, the dynamic of the group shifted and suddenly she was everyone's favorite girl.

Jason and Cadence were the last to leave that night, and while Cadence was talking to Karly about going out to dinner for a double date, Jason looked thoughtful and said, "I'm happy for you, man. She's good for you. I'm sorry I gave you a hard time when I thought she was human. It was hard for me to see you so torn up about your past and possibly making the same mistakes."

"Well, it's also equally hard to get over your past when everyone keeps throwing it up in your face," he smirked, and Jason at least had the decency to look guilty.

"Cades needs a strong female friend that's not a wolf. Someone she can be herself with and not have to be the alpha female. I think your Karly can be that for her, with time." Jason scrubbed fingers across his jaw and looked at the two girls as they leaned against the kitchen counter and talked about restaurants.

"I think I finally understand what made you so crazy all those years. If I had known when I was younger that Karly was meant to be mine but something stood in the way, I think I would have gone insane," Linus said ruefully.

Snorting, Jason rolled his eyes and laughed, "Yeah, well, you were there for me when I needed you, because we're friends not just because we're pack, and some day I'm going to repay that favor for you."

Linus knew he would, even as he hoped he would never have to call in that favor.

Now, watching his friends enjoy the lunch that Karly had prepared for them, knowing she did it not because she was trying to win points with them but because it was just in her nature, he couldn't help but smile and wonder at his good fortune. Fate was a strange and twisted thing.

That weekend, they went out to dinner with Cadence and Jason and had a good time. Cadence seemed eager to have a friend who was as human-appearing as her and not pack, and Karly was – at the core of herself – a very sweet and loving person, willing to accept anyone as a friend that treated her well.

Sunday night, while Karly traced invisible patterns on his back as she cuddled him against her chest after making love, she surprised him. "I need to make an appointment to see a doctor."

His head popped up in alarm. "Are you sick?"

Breathing out a laugh, she smoothed her fingers across his cheek, "No, baby, of course not. My birth control shot is due, and I need to get it done in the next two weeks. Do you...want me to get it?"

He blinked. Was she asking if he was ready for her to have his baby? "Do you want to get it?" He countered.

She hummed in her throat, and her eyes lost focus for a moment, as if she was picturing something in her mind's eye. "It's a quarterly shot, so if I get it in February, then it will be good until the beginning of May.

Depending on when we get married, I'm not against having a child soon if you're ready. I could get it this quarter and then not get it again."

As his emotions fought for dominance, he looked down into her eyes and saw nothing there but love and hope. "I think that sounds like a good plan. I'd at least like to meet your father without you being knocked up."

"So we'll just practice, then."

He growled softly. "Lots of practice."

The full moon approached in that way that sometimes caught him off guard. While his wolf was very in tune with all things lunar, his human self was often scattered enough to not really know which day it was. Just days after Karly and he had talked about having a child together, the full moon took over everything in his world. As fourth, he had a big part in the monthly gathering that included all thirty-eight members of the pack. They met in the lunar clearing that lay a far ways back on the property jointly owned by Cadence and Jason's parents. The house that Jason and Cadence lived in had been owned by her father, who had passed away several years earlier, and the world was a better place without his wolf-hating ass.

The pack would meet at Jason and Cadence's home for a big dinner and then they would meet at the sacred circle and go hunting. Because Cadence was not a true wolf and didn't shift, the wolves would take turns guarding her while Jason went hunting. One full moon, their first together as a real couple, Jason had nearly hurt her very badly because he had not gone hunting and soothed his beast's needs. Linus wasn't going to make that mistake, but he was going to take advantage of the guarded house and have Karly wait there with Cadence for him.

It was bitterly cold when the pack left the house and headed back to the circle before the moon rose for the night. This short time period, she was alone in the house, until pack business was handled and Jason called for everyone to shift and the guards would walk back to the house with Cadence. He'd kissed Karly a dozen times before he left, because he couldn't shake the nerves he was feeling. He just had a feeling that as he got his house of cards stacked up just right that someone would come and blow it all to hell.

When they shifted and howled at the moon, their voices joined in a chorus that was as old as time. Cadence looked him in the eyes and said, "She'll be just fine, Linus. Go hunt."

With those words, he watched the half dozen wolves follow Cadence to the house where his sweetheart was washing dishes after gracing the pack with her amazing cooking skills. If anyone had misgivings about Linus' non-wolf mate, they were bowled over by her food and her smile. Linus was one proud wolf.

He, Jason, Michael, and Bo had spent most of their younger wolf-years hunting together. They were comfortable together and worked as a good team. The woods were dead in the winter in more than one way, which meant that they had to go further to find things, digging rabbits out of holes and finding the occasional deer. In the middle of stalking a small herd of deer, a chorus of wolf howls cut the air, and the four men raised their heads abruptly to listen. It was a call to come back. Something was wrong.

He glanced at Jason, and there was fear in his eyes, too. They raced off a second later, Bo and Michael on their heels. Fuck, he hadn't trusted his gut. He'd known something felt off about the whole night, like there was a bad scent on the air.

The closer they got to the house, the more he cursed the winter hunts and lack of game that made them have to travel so far to curb their needs. But now, his wolf was clamoring in his head to get back to Karly and make sure she was safe. The fear overrode his other needs. Paws pounded on the frozen, snow covered ground. Trees blurred past his peripheral vision. Faster. Faster. She was afraid. He could feel her fear like a bitter taste in the back of his throat, and he surged forward.

Not even bothering to stop, he shifted mid-run and darted into the house to find Karly sitting in the far corner of the couch, clutching his jacket and crying. She fell into his arms as he landed hard on his knees in front of her, burying her face in his neck and weeping. He looked over her head at Cadence who looked very worried.

Jason put his arms around Cadence, and she breathed out a sigh of relief. Linus said, "What's wrong? What happened?"

"There was a wolf, not our pack, in the tree line just after we got back home. I thought it might be one of the teenagers, I haven't really gotten a good look at their hides yet to recognize them," Cadence looked up at Jason, "but Karly recognized him. It's her ex."

Linus felt as confused as Jason looked. He pushed Karly away to arm's length and saw genuine fear in her pretty eyes. It made his wolf bristle. She was not supposed to be afraid ever.

"Sweetheart, who did you see?"

She drew in a gasping, shaky breath and said, "It was Phoenix. From my father's pack."

"Are you certain it was him? It's pretty dark out there." Jason asked, accepting his clothes that another wolf brought for him. Linus' clothes landed near him, but he couldn't think enough to put them on.

Karly nodded, "He's rust brown. It's a color unique to his family line."

"She's right, Jas. I've never seen a wolf that color before. It was almost orange, and he was big." Cadence fidgeted while Jason finished dressing and then leaned back into him for comfort.

"Why is he here?" Jason asked Karly.

She tore her gaze away from Linus'. "I don't know. He's not supposed to be within five hundred yards of me. I have a restraining order against him."

Linus was completely shocked. "Karly, you said he couldn't take a hint. You didn't say he'd been bad enough to require a restraining order."

Jason cleared his throat, "Hold that thought, Linus. Michael, you take a handful of our best trackers and see if you can pick up the trail. Cades will point out where she saw him." Michael nodded and called out a few names, and in just mere seconds, the sound of paws hitting the ground was heard.

Now, in the front room of his alphas' home with only him, Cadence, Jason, Bo, Peter and Tina, Jason's mother, Karly told him her story.

Phoenix Thompson was her playmate and protector. They grew up in the pack together. Several years older than her, he always believed that they were going to be mates when she reached of-age and her angel abilities kicked in. With a hair trigger temper, Phoenix had a tendency to fly off the handle at the slightest thing. He was Karly's first sexual relationship when she was fifteen and he was nineteen. They were together off and on for a few years, and the closer she got to twenty-one, the more possessive he grew. When she turned twenty-one and spent more time with the pack than she had before, testing her powers against the unmated males, Phoenix tried to take out his competition by baiting them into rank fights. He would take the opportunity to maim his opponent instead of having a clean fight, and after a few weeks when Karly was ready to strike out on her own, Phoenix was furious. He promised her that she would belong to him, one way or the other. Under alpha orders to leave her alone, she thought she was safe from him and left.

The first few weeks of her travels, she was fine. She didn't see him and had even stopped thinking about him. And then she went home for the holidays, and after that, she had a sneaking suspicion that she was being followed. When she called home, no one had seen him, and she was encouraged to take care of herself.

Midway through spring, someone started leaving a white rose with her car. Sometimes it was on the windshield, sometimes on the seat. She went back to her home pack for help. Phoenix played innocent, but the alpha ordered him under house arrest and had him punished. Karly once more thought she was safe.

Then, things started happening with her car, which at the time had been a white Camaro. When she went to the police over a slashed tire, he turned more violent and slashed all her tires, broke out her windows, and on one occasion, turned her car upside down in a fit of jealousy when she spent the night at an unmated male's home.

Her home pack sanctioned him and declared him under punishment, except that they didn't know where he was. Her drive to find her mate made her keep pushing, and her father hired a bodyguard to keep an eye on her. He was human, and although strong and a good fighter, after a few weeks of feeling safe for the first time, Phoenix put the man in the hospital and told her she was going to be his no matter what before disappearing again.

"I thought," she sighed and took a deep breath, "I thought that the best thing I could do was find my mate, so I kept pushing forward in my search. My brother Bren sent one of his wolves named Jude to watch over me. He was older, retired military, and for a while I felt like Phoenix was gone. No one had seen or heard from him for weeks. Then Jude got called back home because his mother had died, and that's when Phoenix started to get close again. He set my apartment on fire when I was out with a pack and if I hadn't been too lazy to get my stuff from the car, I would have lost everything. I went home and stayed through the fall, terrified I was never going to be able to leave again. He showed up, though, accepted his punishment, apologized to the pack, and promised he was better. I stayed for a week after his punishment was over. I thought he was getting over me — he even had a female with him that he said changed his life. But then, the night before I was ready to leave on my search again, I woke up in my bedroom and he was on top of me."

She shuddered and Linus' wolf growled. They waited for her to gather herself enough to continue her horrible story. After a few minutes, she did.

She struggled under him, terrified beyond words, and managed to kick him in the groin. When he was doubled over in pain, she screamed for help and got away from him. He snatched her back by her shirt and threw her into the wall, breaking her arm.

By the time she got out of the hospital, the bad news was that he'd managed to survive until dawn and was given his life. The only good news was that their trackers had trailed him up into Canada and believed him gone for good. She had nearly given up searching for her mate, but she was more determined than ever to find the right male for herself and put her past behind her. She stayed through Christmas with her family and started off again. She was weary. Frightened. Determined.

Linus had slipped his jeans on at one point during her story, and he cuddled her against him on the couch. "I just don't understand how he could have found me. Only my parents know where I am. The car is registered to my father. I haven't ever changed my home address on my drivers' license or mail or anything, and I always pay cash."

He kissed the top of her head, "I'll keep you safe, Karly, I swear."

She didn't answer. Whether it was because she already knew that, or because she was afraid to say she didn't think he could, he didn't know. He squeezed her shoulder a little bit tighter and looked at Jason.

Unfortunately this was hitting Cadence a little close to home, and she was trying hard not to lose it. After the other alpha's son had kidnapped her, his plans to rape her and pass her around to his new pack mates still haunted both her and Jason. Jason held her in his arms and met Linus' eyes.

"First things first, let's get Trick over here and make an official report. If he was at the tree line, then he was closer than five hundred yards."

Peter made the call to get Patrick, police chief and human mate of one of their females, to the house. Even though it was very late, he came right away.

Karly told him everything she could about Phoenix. Six feet tall, lean and muscular, brown eyes, white-blonde hair normally kept short, and a scar on the left side of his face down his jaw. Trick said that he would head into the station and run the report, pull up the restraining order, and follow any leads the pack could come up with. By the time he left, Michael and the trackers returned.

From the looks on their faces, it wasn't good. "He's a damn crazy runner. He was all over the place, backtracking, climbing trees and leaping far distances. I've never seen anything like it. He clearly had a vehicle, though, because we lost him just outside town. The trail just stopped abruptly."

Jason wanted some wolves to patrol the woods at Linus' home. It warred with him that he couldn't protect her. Jason clapped his hand on his shoulder, "Your home is about as far removed from the rest of us as possible. There's no protection out there for you. If you want to stay with us, you're welcome to. But as your alpha, I'm telling you that as long as this Phoenix character is out there and looking for her, until we figure out what's going on, you need to be smart. Don't be like me. Don't think you can protect her by yourself, don't take her safety for granted."

Scrubbing his face with his hands, he knew Jason was right. "We'll go stay at my mom's. A half dozen pack members live in her development, and they have security cameras and patrols."

Nodding his approval, Jason sent the patrol over to the development, and Linus said goodnight to them and took Karly home to pack a bag. She seemed lost, shaken, not herself. He knelt in front of her on the bed and took her cold hands in his. "Sweet angel, I promise I will keep you safe. I didn't wait my whole life to find you to have some fuck think he can scare me off. You're mine. Forever."

"I don't want you to get hurt, Linus." Her voice was trembling, a fine shiver of fear in her words.

He straightened and leaned over her, letting his wolf spill out into his eyes so they changed color and his fangs elongated. His voice came out edged with a growl, "You are mine, Karly. I will not let you be taken from me."

Sniffling, she nodded and hugged him.

His mother was waiting for them, the wolves in the development were on alert, and Karly called her father and told him what happened. Linus' first conversation with her father wasn't about marriage and children like he'd wanted it to be.

"Don't take anything for granted with Phoenix. He's unstable," her father Kamren said.

"I won't, sir." He glanced at Karly as she accepted a mug of hot chocolate from his mother. His grandparents had even driven over to the house to offer support.

"When he broke her arm, Linus, I want you to know that I was going to kill him. But the alpha is very traditiona,l and he declared him deserving of pack justice and would forfeit his life if he was caught before dawn. I have never witnessed a wolf confuse an entire pack of males intent on his death, but he was like something possessed. I'm sorry that I let her down."

"I'm going to do everything in my power to keep her safe."

"I know you will. As a wolf with an Angel Mate of my own, I can tell you that there isn't any more powerful mating between two creatures than what you now share with my daughter. I trust you to do your best for her. Perhaps the best thing to do is for you two to make your way up here sooner than March. Maybe getting married will send him packing for good, show that our pack supports you together."

"I'll talk to Karly."

As he hung up, his heart lifted even as it deflated. He would love to marry her tomorrow. But not because of her nutcase ex.

# CHAPTER ELEVEN

"Phoenix," Karly rolled over under the covers with a yawn, "I have class in the morning. You need to go."

"Nah, come on." He tweaked her butt cheek, "Make love to me once more. Please?"

"We've already done it twice, and my dad gets up early, so no." She peeked at him from under the covers, and he scowled but he couldn't keep it up long before he grinned.

"You know what the first thing we're going to do when we're mates is Lynnie?"

"Stop calling me by that nickname?" she said hopefully. He was the only one that had ever called her Lynnie, and she didn't care for it.

"I'll never stop calling you that. No, we're going to go for a nice, long honeymoon. Somewhere warm enough to have the windows open all night and a breeze to keep the room just the right temperature."

She pulled the blanket down far enough to really look at him. Sometimes, he surprised her. He was jaded, hard. He fought his way up from the bottom of the pack and had the battle scars to prove it. He was a punch first, ask questions later sort of man. But there were times, when they were alone, that he showed her the softer side of himself, and this was one of those times.

She stroked the scar on his jaw. It was still angry red and healing from a rank fight the day before. One of the unmated males a handful of years older than her had asked her to have dinner at his house, and she had said yes, only to have him be challenged in a rank fight by Phoenix and then wind up in the hospital. She didn't know why Phoenix was fighting so hard suddenly to move up in the pack, but it was like he was on a mission. "You're a damn romantic when you want to be, Phoenix."

"Just for you. I was thinking maybe we'd spread out in a couple years, make our own pack somewhere. Would you be interested in that?"

She hummed in her throat. "I don't know. Ask me when I'm twenty-one and my angel nature has picked my mate, okay?"

His eyes darkened. "I'm certain we're meant to be mates, Lynnie."

Now his jealous side reared up. "I know you feel that way, Phoenix, and I care about you a great deal, too, but it's not up to me. My nature will choose my perfect mate for me. It's my destiny."

His anger seeped away suddenly, and she recognized the gesture as him trying to control himself for her benefit. "We're perfect together. I love you. I want to spend the rest of my life with you."

"Well, if either of us is going to have a life in the future, then you need to scoot before my dad wakes up." She never told him she loved him, because it wasn't right to say that to him, knowing it was possible he might not be her mate in truth.

"Fine." He groused and then flashed her a winning smile. He pulled on his clothes and leaned over to kiss her. "I'll see you later Lynnie. Sweet dreams." He swung his legs over the window and dropped down two stories to the ground, landing with a bare thud and then the sound of footsteps and then quiet.

* * * *

She woke up and stared at the ceiling. She hadn't given Phoenix much thought since she found Linus. True, she had mentioned that she had a crazy ex, but she hadn't been specific at all because she didn't really think it was anything to mention. Her father's pack had friends at the Canadian border. If he crossed back into the states, they would have been notified. So the questions at the forefront of her brain now were: how had he gotten back, how long had he been back, and just how the hell had he found her? After leaving her parent's home after Christmas, she had gone south immediately because of the weather and stopped for New Year's at a pack in southern Ohio. She hadn't even bothered signing a lease. The pack was entirely mated. After one night, she'd moved on to the pack in Allen and had been in her apartment almost two weeks before Linus found her in the snow.

"Are you thinking about him?" She didn't know how long Linus was up before he spoke.

"Kind of." She looked at him as he went up on one elbow and looked down at her. "I'm sorry that I didn't tell you everything. I would have told you eventually, but I thought he was done with me. I thought I was safe now."

He growled unhappily, and she realized her slip. "No, Linus, no. I'm sorry. I know I'm safe with you, I just mean I thought that, oh hell, I don't know what I thought."

He let out a slow breath. "It's not as if you could have predicted this would happen. Even if I had known the extent of his insanity, I would have believed the same as you; that he was still up in Canada since your dad's pack wasn't notified he tried to cross over. I just...baby I don't want you to be afraid. You are more precious to me than anything else

I've ever known, and I will do my damnedest to keep you safe."

Sincerity poured off him in waves. "I know you will, Linus. I love you."

He pressed a soft kiss to her mouth and whispered against her lips, "I love you, too, angel mine."

Unable to sleep, they lay together for a long, quiet while and eventually just got up. If they were home, she probably would have suggested a nice round of sex to distract them, but aside from not really being in the mood, she just couldn't imagine having sex in his childhood bedroom with his mother and grandparents in the house.

With coffee in their hands, they cuddled on the worn couch in the front room and watched the sun rise over the trees that lined the small street that was part of a gated community for the older generation of wolves. What was most interesting about the Tressel Pack was that when the young wolf alpha Jason took over, the older pack members – his father's generation – stepped down.

"Why is that weird? Isn't it normal for the best ones to be the top ranked?"

"Well, sure, but you said they just stepped down. They were barely middle age, and they just walked away from leading. The second in command didn't take over leadership or fight Michael for his position, right?"

"No." He looked at her in silence for a moment. "I never gave it any thought. The pack has always been led by a Gerrick. Are there any wolves your age ranked high in your dad's pack?"

"Hell no," she laughed. "The alpha is a vicious fighter and so are all his highly ranked men. And anyway, if someone wanted to take over, he'd have to fight his way up, and besides my father's passionate study of martial arts giving him an edge, the third ranked is a pro boxer in the were-circuit and the fourth ranked is a retired Navy Seal. When my father was fighting his way up the ranks back when he was young, he said that the only reason that he made it to second is because the alpha arranged them himself after a fight between the three of them that showed them to be evenly matched in strength and determination. It's been that way for decades, and it works for them."

"Wow, I'd probably be low man on the totem pole with your dad's pack."

"It wouldn't matter to me anyway. The pack is very traditional, and many of the younger generation my age leave after a few years to find less restrictive packs. The alpha's son is hopeful that by the time his dad is ready to step down that the entire old guard will be ready to also step down so he can take over, but unless my dad is too old to lead, then he doesn't have a prayer."

"I never really thought about it, but I guess the way things happened in our pack isn't normal at all. When Peter got injured and Jason took over in interim, none of the older wolves questioned him, and when he stood up to take over full time, there were no challenges. When rank fights were initiated, they all stepped back. The former second, Peter's right hand Henry, told me once that he had fifteen years as second and thought that was plenty long enough to keep young wolves in line. He wanted to enjoy his grandkids without having to deal with pack responsibility." He sighed and went quiet for a moment.

"Karly, there's something your dad said that I wanted to run by you." He put their mugs down on the coffee table and turned to face her. Taking her hand in his, he twisted the ring on her finger. "Your father suggested we come up to see them and get married. He said that perhaps showing the pack's support of our marriage would show Phoenix that it's time for him to move on."

She ran the back of her hand across his cheek. "You don't really look thrilled with the prospect."

"No, baby, I do want to marry you. If we do this right now because we're trying to send a message, then it's like he's forcing our hands. I'm not really crazy about giving him that much power."

She chewed the inside of her lip. Yes, she wanted to marry Linus, but he was right. It seemed almost like a last ditch effort to keep Phoenix off their backs. And then they'd always know that the timing was born of violence.

"Well, you know, there's an angel mating ceremony. My mother would oversee it. It's kind of like the wolf ceremony, done in front of the pack. My mother always expected to do it twice, once for my home pack so that my mate would be welcome as an honored friend and once with my new pack like a joining ceremony. If we went up to my parents' pack and did the angel ceremony, that's as good as being married to them and will give us something like an alliance with that pack. For both of us."

"Yeah? That's pretty cool." He scrubbed his fingers along his jaw. "Are you okay with that?"

"Sure. I want you to meet my parents and my home pack. When we went up for our visit in March she probably would have wanted to do it anyway to bind us all together as family. It's important to angels that their girls are happy and their mates are welcome in their pack. My parents were in the same pack, they grew up together, so the angel mating ceremony was done at the same time as the pack joining ceremony and the legal marriage."

She explained the ceremony was done at sunrise, so the world would look new on the mated pair, and that ancient and sacred prayers of her kind were spoken over the couple that were draped in orange blossoms, signifying a sweet life. Then the males of the pack would embrace the couple to commit their scent to memory, so that if help was called for, they would be able to find both and support them. The females of the pack would bring mating gifts for the couple of prepared hides and blankets for their new home, and then the male would go on a hunt with his angel's pack and the kills would be brought back for a feast that would last until midnight. Then the mated couple left to spend the night together in the home of her mother. That signified the mother and father supported the daughter and her mate in the first steps of their life together.

"It's really incredible," he murmured, cuddling her into his side. "I had no idea how much we were all missing out on because of the modernization of our pack. You make me want things to be different."

"Just because your pack is modern doesn't mean that you have to raise our children that way, and I want our family to embrace the laws and the spirit of the old ways. Our sons are going to be alphas. We have to prepare them for that burden."

"And our daughters will be Angels," he added, kissing the tip of her nose with a soft smile. "They have to be prepared for that, too."

"I've always thought that Peter was the detriment of the pack," a rumbling voice said behind them, and they both turned around in surprise to see Linus' grandfather, known as Pops, leaning heavily on his cane in the doorway.

"Pops?" Linus questioned.

"Well," his grandfather drawled, "Abraham, Peter's father, was one of the most powerful alphas I've ever had the pleasure of knowing. When his wife was shot and killed by a hunter, he was paralyzed, devastated by the loss and unable to handle his duties as alpha. Peter took over, partly out of fear that the other males in the pack might try to take him out and that he was in such deep grief that he would just give up and go to the grave. But also, partly because he didn't want the pack to splinter under poor leadership. Peter is powerful enough to be alpha, but he didn't have the drive for it...hunger, I guess, is the right word. He didn't want to spend the time teaching the pups about the old ways because he had never wanted to follow them himself. And then he was injured, and Jason took over. He's a good alpha, because the pack is safe in its territory and relatively small, but if another pack ever really came against us, I shudder to think what might happen."

Linus tensed, and his voice was edged in defense. "He proved his ability to lead when he hunted down and killed the rogue that kidnapped Cadence."

"Yes, out of necessity. But that wasn't pack business, Linus, not entirely. That male took his mate. Ask yourself if Jason would spend all night chasing a rogue for one of the lesser wolves' human mates or an unmated female?"

He opened his mouth and then he sighed, "How can I teach my own children things I barely know myself?"

"Our family will help you, Linus," Pops said with a gentle smile. "And I'm certain that Karly's family will be more than happy to share all they know. It's about time that some grandpups scampered around this dusty old place." His eyes twinkled in happiness before he turned and moved slowly out of the room.

She smiled at the empty space where he had stood. "Are your grandparents still alive?" he asked, turning her gently by the shoulder to face him.

"No, my mother's parents were quite a bit older by the time she was born. They lived into their late 80s and died within a few years of each other. I have some memories of my grandmother, but they're very faint. And my father's parents died when I was a teenager. What about your dad's parents? Are they still here with this pack?"

Every feature in his face changed from curiosity at their conversation to unhappiness in a blink. "We should get something to eat for breakfast and then make arrangements with your parents to do the angel mating ceremony."

He nearly ran out of the room and left her sitting there in surprise.

Unfortunately, they really didn't have time to deal with his demons, since her own were blood and flesh and stalking her. She wasn't sure if she entirely believed that doing the angel mating ceremony would change Phoenix's mind about her, but being around her family and the pack might. She could hope, anyway.

Linus' mother made breakfast while Karly talked to her mother about the mating ceremony. They decided to wait a few days to see if Phoenix would show himself again before they headed to West Virginia, and they would plan to spend a few weeks there on an extended vacation. Linus' family was going to join them, and after a few phone calls, the third ranked of the pack, Bo, was going to come with them, along with a few of their lesser-ranked wolves and the former alpha Peter and his wife, Tina. Linus and her father both believed in safety in numbers, and they would only stay for the ceremony and celebration and then head home the following day. Her parents, along with members of the pack, would escort them back home unless Phoenix showed himself and was dealt with.

She didn't even want to think about that. She knew that wolves were fiercely protective of their mates, but she'd also seen Phoenix fight, and there was no telling what this time apart had done to him, how he'd trained and changed. If he was unbalanced before, he could be a total fruit loop at this point. A dangerous one, but a fruit loop nonetheless.

Aside from talking to her mother about the orange blossom garland for the ceremony, there wasn't anything that had to be prepared special until the males went hunting. Karly had heard the story about her parents' mating time, and how her mother had waited for her mate to come back to her after he hunted. Karly had always pictured the angel mating ceremony in her mind and was thrilled that it was going to happen so soon, even as a tickling warning in the back of her mind told her that it wasn't going to be the be-all and end-all of their problems with her ex. She was just not that lucky.

# CHAPTER TWELVE

Stroking down the soft curve of Karly's waist, Linus pressed his mouth to hers and pulled her closer. They were leaving in the morning to head to her father's pack in West Virginia. All the plans were in place, and everyone was ready to get his mate safely to her parents' pack and mated by angel standards before they headed home. He was nervous to meet her parents and be under the watchful eye of an alpha that expected wolves to know their history and laws, but he was also grateful to be taking her someplace that held her safety in such esteem. With her father as second of the pack, he knew that every male there would be patrolling for that bastard Phoenix.

Yesterday he took her home so they could pack and then she sat in the shop while he closed up his workspace and handed off his jobs for the next few weeks. He felt like they were running away from the problem, but every time he mentioned his feelings, she promised him that she didn't feel that way. It warred with his beast that she felt a kernel of unease in her mind. He should be able to protect her. She should have no doubt that he could keep her safe from harm — and not just her but their future children.

Karly's whispered voice teased his ear, "If we make love, your family's going to hear, and I just don't think I can handle that."

Underneath the edge of her satin panties, he felt the warmth of her body as it heated for him. They hadn't made love in two days. If his family hadn't come to his house with them while they packed, he would have pounded Karly through the mattress to make up for everything.

He licked the edge of her jaw, and she shivered. "What if I promise to go very, very slow?" His finger traced the seam of her sex, her silky honey coating the tip of his finger.

"Slow's not the problem," she breathed.

"No?" He chuckled.

"No, it's, oh, Linus," she moaned softly, dragging her teeth over her lower lip as he slid his finger inside her heat. The scent of her arousal spiked in the air, and his already hard cock turned to stone against her side. He could guess she was worried about what his family would think about their lovemaking, that she didn't want to be embarrassed. She should know better, though. His mother was so happy for them, and his grandparents were, too. And wolves were notoriously horny. No one in the house would think twice about them enjoying each other and this small bit of time alone.

He felt her legs tense as she tried to resist spreading her luscious thighs to give him better access, but a press of his thumb to her already swollen clit made them slide apart and he buried his finger inside her. Keeping his thumb tight on her little pleasure button, he added a second finger, twisting it in his search for that one place that would rocket her to the heavens. She wiggled under him, her eyes closed and her nails digging in his shoulder. A heartbeat before she came, he clamped his hand over her mouth, and she screamed into his palm, her back arching off the bed in pure ecstasy.

Her body rocked on the bed, making it shake and creak but she was too lost to the sensations to notice. He rolled on top of her, tearing her panties off with one hand and guiding his cock inside her. He gripped her ankles and brought them up to his shoulders so that her legs were locked together and straight, her channel perfectly tight and hot around him. After a few experimental thrusts, she groaned at the position, and he gave her a devilish smile and bit down on the arch of her foot.

With such sensitive feet, his angel whimpered and ground her teeth together while he thrust into her to drive them both to the edge and over. He felt the tremors in her belly as another orgasm bloomed to life in her, and he pulled her ankles away from his shoulders and spread her legs high and wide apart so he could watch his cock disappear into the depths of her body. Completely at his mercy, she clutched at the blankets on the bed and whimpered and moaned. She was just made so perfectly for him; he couldn't get enough of her. Sweat dotted his brow as he watched himself hammer into her willing pussy, oblivious to everything except the sound of her breathing and the hitch in her throat when she came. Her body squeezed him tight and he groaned, dropping her legs and going into a pushup over her to power the last few thrusts to his own climax.

She pulled him down, and he took the brunt of his weight on his arms and settled into the cradle of her body. She kissed his cheek with a feather light touch and hugged him tightly. "You come so hard, baby, it's like you'll break my cock in half."

She breathed out a chuckle and tilted his face to kiss him on the mouth. "It's because you love me so well, my sweet wolf."

Eventually his arms protested the angle at which he was holding himself away from her body, so he rolled to his back and pulled her with him to cuddle into his chest. "My heart," she said with a light yawn.

"It's beating just for you, baby," he promised and closed his eyes.

Armed with directions, their caravan left Allen at 7:30 in the morning on February 3. In the back of the truck were their two suitcases, and her angel book and camera equipment. She was determined to take a picture of him in the snow in his shift, and they'd not had an opportunity to do it before now.

Peter and Tina drove his mother and grandparents in their minivan and led the way. Behind them, Bo and the rest of the wolves followed in two vehicles. Bo had been curious if there were any single females in the pack, and Karly said that most of the females her age were already mated or had moved to other packs to escape the alpha's rule. Unlike their own pack, the alpha female, while powerful, wasn't the boss of anyone and fell under her mate's thumb just as any other wolves did. Karly had thought it was odd that the males and females in the Tressel Pack had their own hierarchy. For her parents' pack, the females were not ranked, they were meant to be mates and supportive of their males. When he told her he thought it was slightly on the barbaric side and not at all in keeping with women's lib and the like, she had just shrugged.

"All packs are different, Linus. None of them are entirely right, and the only thing that keeps the wolves in the pack is their freedom of choice. Alpha Krayne runs the pack with an iron fist and has fought for their territory alongside his people many times. There are females that think they should have a say in the politics of the pack and should be thought of as more than mates and mothers and caretakers, but they're free to leave. It's all I've ever known, and besides the fact that I was born to be a wolf's mate, his leadership has saved the lives of nearly every wolf in the pack more than once."

"You don't have to defend the pack's way of life to me, Karly," he picked her hand up and kissed the back of it.

"I'm not trying to. I'm not a wolf so the politics of your pack don't interest me. What does interest me is you being happy and our children growing up with a love for what they will be and the desire to see harmony and law within their pack."

"I want that, too." And he did. While they both allowed the subject to drop, he couldn't help but think about how inadequate he felt in going to her old pack. He was worried he'd make a complete jackass of himself and embarrass her.

Three hours into their drive, Peter called on his cell to say that all the women in the minivan needed a bathroom break even though they hadn't planned to stop for lunch for another hour. It sounded like complete anarchy over the phone so Linus had no trouble agreeing to stop. He knew just how feisty his grandmother could be, and if she wanted to stop, she'd crawl over Peter and put her foot on the brake herself.

The rest area in Ohio was surrounded by woods and a small clearing with picnic tables. The building was brick and typical, with one side for women to enter and the other for men. Another glass building housed vending machines.

Parting with Karly at the juncture of the two sidewalks, he kissed her briefly and watched her follow his mother, grandmother and Tina around the corner and into the bathroom.

Lowering his zipper at the urinal, he sighed and rolled his neck. He was tense in more than one way. "So, do you think her folks will like you?" Bo asked from next to him.

"I hope so. She said the only way that they wouldn't like me is if she'd ignored her nature and just picked someone to be with."

"It's wicked cool, man." Bo sighed. "That she was made for you."

"I know, I'm really lucky. I really thought I blew my chance at happiness before, but it turns out that I didn't really know what happy was until I met Karly."

He joined the men out at the vehicles after grabbing sodas for himself and Karly. No one was in a hurry to get back on the road so they chatted about the trip and stopping for lunch and meeting the pack.

Glancing at his watch for the hundredth time, he looked at Peter. "They've been in there for ten minutes. This place isn't so busy that they would be standing in line."

"Maybe they're just talking." Pops said, "Your grandmother could talk a monk into breaking his vows if only to tell her to be quiet."

He chuckled but it was forced. Suddenly, he felt like something wasn't quite right. He met Peter's eyes again, and Peter said, "We'll, um, holler into the bathroom for them to hurry up."

They walked together as a group, and as they rounded the corner, he opened the door a few inches and said, "Karly? Baby, are you okay?"

Silence followed. Frowning, he opened the door further, and a woman he didn't know looked at him from the sink. "Do you need something?" she asked.

"Yeah, my fiancé came in here like ten minutes ago with a few other women."

"It's just me in here, but three of the stalls are locked with people in them." She shrugged and walked past him. He stormed into the bathroom and pushed one of the closed doors but the lock just rattled.

Peter and his grandfather both joined him, and Bo stuck his head in, "Linus, Teller is freaking out. He says he can smell that rust wolf around here. Is Karly okay?"

His wolf snarled in his brain, and he smashed the flat of his palm on the door, breaking the metal lock apart as it opened. Tina lay slumped on the toilet, her head resting on the wall. "Oh no," he breathed, darting his hand to her neck. Relief washed through him as the other doors popped open, and his mother and grandmother were found in a similar position. Drugged into unconsciousness but otherwise unharmed.

He ran out of the bathroom to leave them to tend to the women and found Teller, a young wolf and one of their best trackers, growling and flexing his hands like his claws wanted to break free. At the back of the small building, a service door had been broken, and a man in a janitorial uniform lay dead inside from a broken neck. Inside the small service room was another door that led to the women's restroom. It's clearly how Phoenix got inside.

He shut the door on the dead body and closed his eyes. Bo pressed his hand on his shoulder and handed him something. It was Karly's shoe. "Teller found it at the tree line, and I brought it back for you."

Linus took the shoe and squeezed it in his hands and let loose a howl of rage that the others echoed.

Phoenix took his mate! He would suffer slowly when he was found.

# CHAPTER THIRTEEN

She had the worst headache ever. She tried to roll over so she could get up and get some aspirin, but something on her wrist tugged and prevented it. She pulled harder, and the feel of something enclosing her wrist made her try to force her eyes open. She was met with a wooden ceiling that didn't look at all familiar, and dropping her slightly blurry vision to her arm, she saw that her wrist was tied with a thick length of rope to an iron headboard. The knot had been pushed down to the mattress, and there was a foot of rope between her wrist and the headboard.

Fear spiked through her as a door creaked open, and she jerked up but was prevented from doing anything but scooting against the headboard as her eyes found the door with Phoenix walking through it, a paper grocery sack in one arm.

His eyes lit up when he saw her. "Hey, you're awake!" He kicked the door shut and put the sack down on a tiny kitchen table and walked towards her.

She screamed, "Stay back!"

He paused, and quirked his brow and then kept walking, sitting on the end of the bed. "How do you feel?"

"Why am I here? Where am I?" Panic clawed at her throat, and she tried to tamp it down. She focused on slowing her breathing to calm her racing heart.

"You're here because you belong to me, Lynnie. And where you are isn't as important as why. Because you're mine. We belong together. I told you that when we were kids, and I've let you have your fun playing around with other wolves, but enough is enough."

"No, Phoenix. It's not as if I chose this life. I have to follow my nature. You're not my mate, or I would have chosen you right away. You've known that all along."

His pleasant smile disappeared as if someone poured hot water over his face and melted it into a severe frown. Standing abruptly, he snatched the hair at the side of her head and jerked her off the bed until her arm wrenched painfully against the rope. "You. Are. Mine." Releasing her so she bounced hard on the mattress, she sobbed loudly at the pain where he'd pulled strands of hair free in his anger and gritted her teeth together until she could quiet the waves of despair that threatened.

He went back into the kitchen and unloaded the supplies from the paper sack. Groceries. A few loaves of bread, peanut butter, jelly, and bottled water. She looked around while he put the things away. It looked like a one-room cabin. Everything was made of wood, from the floor to the ceiling. If there were windows, they were boarded up now. There were three doors. One that led outside that he'd come through, and two others. A bathroom and...a closet maybe? Or another bedroom? The furnishings were dusty from disuse. A worn couch against the wall looked over a large stone fireplace. There was a small kitchen table and chairs and a short counter by the sink and stove.

"Like what you see, Lynnie? I found this empty cabin when I first was scouting a place for our honeymoon. No one's been here in years, but even if there'd been a whole family here, it wouldn't have mattered. It would be empty now." Phoenix sat down and smoothed her hair away from her face. She flinched, and he gave her a sad smile. "Aw, don't be like that. I can't have you trying to get away from me over some ridiculous thing like destiny. You and I were meant for each other, and now that I have you, I'm never going to let you go."

She licked her dry lips. "How did you, how did you bring me here?" Her thoughts flashed to Linus, to his family and friends. Had Phoenix killed them all to get her? She couldn't remember anything after kissing Linus goodbye at the rest stop.

A smug smirk crossed his thin lips. "Ah, that was easy. I masked my scent using some strong deer musk and watched your activities for the last few days. When you were heading back to West Virginia, I knew that you'd hide out there with the old pack because your pathetic cub of a boyfriend can't handle me." Snorting, he relaxed and leaned over her legs. "Anyway, I just followed you, figuring you'd stop eventually and the rest area was perfect. I broke in through a back service door and waited until you were all in the stalls, and then I tossed in a little bomb. It was a potion mixed in a thin glass vial. It knocks anything out in less than two seconds and spreads incredibly fast in small areas like that. Caught everyone with their pants down." He laughed and patted her thigh like it was a big joke. Her heart dropped into her stomach.

"Anyway, I grabbed you from the stall after pulling your pants back up and carried you through the back door and into the woods. Had my car waiting on a service road, put you in the trunk, and they didn't know what hit them, that's for damn sure."

"What are you going to do to me, Phoenix?"

"Do?" He sat up and loomed over her, his eyes wild. "I'm going to mate with you, Lynnie, so we'll be together forever."

She stared at him in shock. He was completely delusional. Fear trickled through her again, and he closed his eyes and took in a deep breath. "Ah, that smells great. You should be afraid, because I'm pretty pissed at you for walking away from me. And spare me about your fate and all that bullshit. You're mine, and I'll kill you before I let you go." She knew that was as true a statement as any that she'd ever heard.

He gave her a long look. "I know he won't choose her over you, Lynnie. But I know you'll choose her over freedom, so you're not going anywhere. She's my little insurance policy."

She looked at him in confusion, but before she could ask him who he was talking about, he crossed the small room and opened one of the two doors revealing a small closet and, to her surprise, Brenda, Linus' ex was tied up, gagged, and totally freaked out. She whimpered as she sat in the tiny space, and Phoenix looked down at her as if she were not a person but something insignificant like a pair of old shoes. Her throat tightened. She knew the look in her eyes spoke volumes to what she'd suffered already at his hands. She had a black eye. There were probably more bruises she couldn't see. And the simple fact that she didn't appear to have clothes on at all made Karly's eyes sting with tears. Dirty, disheveled. How long had he had her?

"Why do you have Linus' ex-wife, Phoenix?"

"She's the one that contacted me." He continued to look down at Brenda, and she started to hyperventilate. "I could take her; show you how submissive I like my women now. Would you like that, Lynnie?" He looked up at Karly, and the man staring back at her was a virtual stranger.

"I don't want to watch you rape her." Her voice trembled and she tried to keep the fear away, but it was damn, damn hard.

He snorted and slammed the door shut. "Can't rape a willing accomplice. She wanted me to get you out of the way, and I snagged her two days ago and have been keeping myself busy with her. She tried to escape, so I had to tie her up. But," he shrugged and sat down next to Karly again, "that didn't stop me from playing with her. I could let you play with her. I think I'd enjoy watching her eat your pussy, Lynnie. Maybe while I fuck her."

Karly's eyes went wide, and she wondered how she'd been so devastatingly wrong about him. He was so casual. So cruel without thought, like some kind of mindless robot. She knew her best defense was to get on his good side so he would let his guard down and she could escape. Brenda was a complication for sure, and she didn't want to leave her behind. He had her by the scruff.

She tried not to jerk on the tie around her wrist. "I don't, I don't remember you being so aggressive, like this, Phoenix."

His brow arched, and a sneer pulled up half his mouth. "I was vanilla for you because it's what you wanted, what you would tolerate. That," he gestured towards the closet, "is what I've always enjoyed. There were some she-wolves from another pack that I used to fuck around with back then so I didn't go crazy being so boring in bed with you. You'll learn soon enough that pain for pleasure's sake can be quite enjoyable. At least in my opinion."

Her poor heart stuttered to a dead stop, and her breath seized in her chest. When a jolt made her come back to awareness again, she blinked hard to keep the tears away and said, "Was all of it a lie? All those sweet promises in the dark in my bed?"

The sneer deepened. "Maybe. Maybe not. We could have kept things like that for our whole lives. Vanilla for you and not-even-close-to-vanilla for me with other she-wolves. Perhaps if you hadn't walked away from me, if you'd believed me to be your mate in truth, then I wouldn't have indulged my darkest fantasies for the last year and a half. Now, I don't think I could even get it up for vanilla."

The sneer disappeared, and he stood up and walked over to the small kitchen. "I'll make you something to eat, I'm sure you're hungry, Lynnie."

She gaped at his back. It was like someone had flipped a switch. Sadistic rapist one minute, kind hearted gentleman the next. He looked over his shoulder, "Are you hungry?"

Remembering her plan to get him to let his guard down so she could get free, she licked her dry lips and nodded, "Yes, Phoenix, thank you."

"I take care of my girl. I remember how you liked to eat peanut butter and strawberry jelly sandwiches. I made sure to get what you liked, so I don't have to risk taking you out of the woods anytime soon."

While his back was turned at the counter, she inspected the knot that bound her wrist to the headboard. It was a double knot of some kind. She wiggled her wrist back and forth, and it could move but was not loose enough for her to even consider trying to pull her wrist through. And she knew if she tried, that her wrist would swell and then she'd be even more miserable. Keeping an eye on Phoenix's back, she worked at the knot, stopping just as he turned towards her.

He sat next to her on the bed and put a paper plate in her lap with two peanut butter and jelly sandwiches in it and held a bottle of water up to her mouth. She reached for it with her free hand, but he knocked it away. "I'll take care of you, Lynnie."

Accepting the water, she drank half before he pulled it away and then tugged a corner of the sandwich off and held it up to her mouth. She *so* didn't want to be hand-fed by a nutcase, but she couldn't exactly do anything about that so she opened her mouth dutifully and let him place the wedge on her tongue. In truth, she didn't really have much of an appetite. She hadn't, really, since she saw his wolf form outside of Jason and Cadence's house. That seemed like an eternity ago.

"Do you remember, Lynnie, when we found that small creek near the lunar meeting place and made love on the bank?"

"I remember almost getting busted by the alpha." She smiled at him even though it was the last thing she wanted to do.

"That was a long time ago. A lifetime." He quieted as he fed her the rest of the sandwich and the last of the water. He ate the other sandwich and then put the plate in the trash.

Phoenix was on edge, bouncing on his heels as he wavered between talking about their past and their future. Every opportunity that he turned his back to her, she worked on the knot, millimeters coming free and filling her heart with hope.

She wondered where they were. She wondered how long she'd been unconscious. She wondered how long it was before Linus realized something was wrong. For the thousandth time she shouted Linus' name in her head and begged him to find her.

Phoenix lit a match in front of the stone fireplace. Sulfur filled the air for a moment as he knelt down. Crumpled newspaper flared to life underneath a stack of wood that began to crackle. She tugged on the knot while he was absorbed in the fire.

"I thought," he said, turning around, "that you would prefer me to burn off the tattoo on your shoulder over cutting it off with my hunting knife? And then there's the business of your marks from your former mate, those will also have to go."

*Holy shit.*

She swallowed hard and opened her mouth, but words failed to come out. His brow cocked, "Would you rather me cut them off you? I will, but I'd think a burn would be less devastating than me slicing a few layers of skin off. If I cut your skin open with a knife, it's going to make my wolf go nuts with all that blood, and I might not be able to control what happens after that. What do you think?"

Finding her voice, she squeaked, "It won't change anything, Phoenix. The tattoo is just a part of my history, it isn't where my power comes from, and the marks are only a symbol not the source of love for my mate."

He moved across the room and climbed up onto the bed. "I am not an idiot; I know that. I simply do not want to see them or ever be reminded of the reason that you left me. I'm going to get rid of them tonight, and while you recover for a while, I'm going to fuck that human at least once more before I kill her. Then you and I will celebrate our first night as mates, our honeymoon."

Tears stung, and she nearly drowned in the wave of helplessness that threatened to crash over her. Phoenix had completely lost his mind. She found some strength, buried deeply underneath that fresh taste of fear, and said, "You can let Brenda go. You got me. You got what you wanted. She doesn't have to die."

He grunted and climbed closer to her, gripping her chin between his fingers. "Of course she has to die. She knows my face, my name, hell even how to get in touch with me. She's very resourceful, and on top of that, she's also pretty evil. She knew what I'd done to you and still she called for me, practically drew a map on how to get to that pack's lunar meeting place so I could find you and take you with me. She just didn't know that I planned to also take her along for insurance. She's outlived her usefulness, though. She'll be my bachelor party. And the bonus is that you get a front row seat to how I like to fuck now. I won't go so hard on you this first time, but I'll warm you up to what I like in time."

"How did you...how did she find you if no one knew where you were?"

He shrugged and played with a loose string on the blanket. "She sent a letter to the address in the DMV file. It showed up at my old rental house in West Virginia, and the guy that rented it after me sent it to the owner of the house who looked up my emergency contact who happened to be my cousin Eddie. You remember him, don't you?" He paused until she nodded. Eddie was two years younger than her and not playing with a full deck of cards.

"Well, he had instructions to send anything he got for me to a PO box up in Canada and to keep his mouth shut. When I got the letter, I shipped a box of clothes down to a motel near that pitiful excuse for a wolf pack, and then I shifted and crossed the border. It's why no one knew I came back down to the states; they were looking for Phoenix

Thompson, not a rust-colored wolf. I ran in my shift all the way down to Kentucky. The box was waiting for me in a room that I'd rented ahead of time, and I found some clothes so I could check into the room. Then I met up with Brenda and began to plan how to get you."

She sure didn't like the way he said he found clothes. It sounded like someone had been killed for their pants. She shivered and swallowed against the permanent lump in her throat. Her palms were sweating, and her eyes stung with tears.

"So, branding or knife? Ladies choice."

His face was expectant like a child at Christmas. She stared in his blue-blue eyes and knew that she'd die by his hand someday. Maybe not today, but sometime in the future, he would kill her. She'd never faced her own death before.

She hadn't wanted to give up hope, but in a short amount of time, Phoenix was going to get rid of the reminders of what she really was, and then rape and kill Brenda before he raped and did who knows what else to her. She didn't know the meaning of the word hope anymore when she said, "Burn."

He nodded, kissed her cheek and climbed off the bed. As he turned to tend the fire, she worked frantically on the knot. While he'd been spouting off his insanity, she'd made the decision to free herself and leave if she could. She was certain that if she could free herself and if she could get out of the house, that he wouldn't kill Brenda and she could get help for both of them. There was just no way to free both of them, not that she could see. She didn't want to be the girl that ran out on someone who needed help, but if she couldn't get free, then they were both as good as dead.

She watched him, moving her hand to her stomach instead of at the knot when he turned back around, rummaged in a large duffel on the couch, and pulled out a long handled object that was dark gray like it was made out of iron. It ended in a small, flat disc. He met her eyes and walked over to her. Running his finger across the smooth bottom of the circle, he said, "I had a plain brand made especially for this occasion. I'll heat it red hot in the fire, and it will melt that tattoo off your shoulder in a blink. A painful blink, but still, pretty damn quick. And as far as those old marks go, it's wide enough to cover them, but I'll probably have to do it twice to get all four."

If he was waiting for her approval, she couldn't think past what looked like a huge object he was going to shove into her skin. He waved it at her a little, smiled, and then walked over to the fire. He angled the end of the brand into the fire and leaned his free hand against the mantel, seemingly lost in thought. Again she snapped to careful motion and worked on the knot. She finally got the tip of her finger underneath one of the loops and pulled, and it slid free. She would have hollered for joy if it wouldn't have been the stupidest thing on record.

She saw his muscles tense, and she stopped moving just seconds before he turned and walked over to the closet. The door opened, and he bent down to pick up Brenda. She fought him. He had apparently only gagged and bound her wrists not her ankles. Karly saw her feet kick out, and she screamed through the gag. He cursed, scrambling to get to her past her kicks.

The second loop caught on something, and her heart threatened to burst in her chest. She cast a side glance down to her wrist and saw that it was simply twisted so it wouldn't pull free without an opposite twist. Keeping her eyes dead ahead of her and watching as he grabbed Brenda by the hair on the top of her head and pulled her screeching in pain to her feet, Karly freed the last part of the knot. Her wrist moved freely now, and she dropped her hand back to her stomach and watched in horror as he dragged Brenda bodily to the bed.

He threw her next to Karly and held her immobile with his hand on her throat while he rummaged around on the floor for something. Metal rattled and clinked and he pulled out handcuffs and secured her wrists together, anchoring them high at the top of the headboard. Her eyes bulged and her face turned purple, and Karly said, "Phoenix, please, she can't breathe!"

With an annoyed grunt, he released her neck and secured her ankles to the opposite corners of the bed so she was spread wide open. Karly had to pull her legs up to make room for her. She looked away the instant she saw dried blood on her thighs and fought crying. She steeled herself against the fear and sorrow and painful finality that came to her and looked at the front door. The only way out of the cabin. Phoenix had made the mistake of not locking the door, clearly trusting that she would be unable to free herself.

"Do you want to use the bathroom before we get started?" Phoenix asked her. She panicked for an instant, knowing he'd see that she had undone the knot.

She spoke without thinking, glad that some part of her brain was on autopilot. "I'm good, sw-sweetie. A full bladder during sex makes the orgasms much better."

His eyes widened, and he grinned, "So my sweet Lynnie has learned some new tricks?"

"It sounds like you have, too." She smiled, forcing the shakiness from her voice.

"Okay, brand first and then the human and then we'll see where the night takes us." He leaned over Brenda and patted her cheek, "You'll be dead by dawn, bitch. No one plays my woman for a fool or uses me like you tried to."

Brenda whimpered, tears staining her dirty face, and her wild look was both apologetic and frantic. Phoenix smiled at her and then turned and walked to the fireplace. The rope slipped free with a twist of her hand. The moment he was as far away from the door as possible and distracted, she raced towards the front door. Twisting the doorknob, she wrenched the door open and burst through to the porch. She heard

Phoenix's surprised shout but was already off the porch and running. Phoenix yelled at her, just a few steps behind her as she raced out into the dark woods.

Fear like something alive bit at the back of her neck like rabid dogs as she ran for her life, blindly, not sure where she was going or how long she could run without shoes. The woods were dark; the moon a bare sliver. Branches slapped at her as she ran. Phoenix yelled for her, calling her name amongst threats of killing her if she didn't come back to him immediately and promises of not punishing her for running away.

"Lynnie, Lynnie. Don't be like this." he said with a sweet, loud voice.

Her pulse thundered in her ears, and she pushed herself faster. If she stopped running, she was as good as dead.

"You'll be sorry you ran, little girl." His voice was a growl now, angry and demanding.

*Linus, Linus! I need you, please!*

Darting through trees, she could barely see. Phoenix taunted, "I like a good chase, Lynnie, but we've got work to do. Come back to me now, and I'll forget you tried to leave me again."

She stumbled through a clearing, and her foot caught on an above ground root. She tumbled, smashing shoulder-first into a thick tree. She cried out at the sharp, separate pains as she fell forward. Tears spilled from her eyes as she caught herself with her good hand on the ground and rolled to her butt. She backed against a large tree and pressed herself into the shadows, even though she knew it wouldn't matter. Phoenix would find her and kill her now. Her ankle throbbed, and her shoulder hurt. Even in the midst of the pain, she wasn't sorry for herself but for Linus.

She wished she could leave a note for her sweet mate to tell him how much he meant to her, how much she loved him, and how sorry she was that she had let him down. She sobbed loudly, unable to stop herself, as dead branches crackled around her and a low, deep growl rumbled in the night air.

This was how her life was going to end.

# CHAPTER FOURTEEN

He felt her fear like a tangible thing, a creature twisting and writhing in his belly as he drove. Their engines cut the quiet night like chainsaws, like birds of prey with growls of rage, poised to attack. He was running on pure instinct, talking directly to the beast part of himself so they could find their mate and bring her home safe. His wolf was so in tune with his mate that he could feel her on the air, like a compass needle pointing to north.

The road ended abruptly into woods, and he turned off the bike and got off, running his hands through his hair and closing his eyes. He let his beast loose further, scenting the air for her uniquely sweet scent, but couldn't smell her. He could feel her, though. She was just too far for scent.

"Which way?" Jason asked, coming to stand next to him. Linus glanced at his alpha and friend. His grandfather had been wrong. When Linus called Jason in a panic, he was on his way within minutes, the pack at his back. The pack had met up with them as they'd headed southwest. Michael had ridden Linus' bike up so Linus could use the air to try to scent for her. They were near the border of Kentucky, south of Cincinnati.

Without opening his eyes, he started walking, taking a step to the left and entering the woods. "This way."

He walked slowly at first, going with his wolf, listening to the sounds of the forest and hoping for a sound or sign that someone had brought his mate through here. With his heightened senses, he could see almost as clear as if it were daytime. Jason instructed several wolves to shift and scout ahead. Bo said, "Hey, I'm looking at an aerial map of the area here, and there's a cabin about a mile this direction."

Bo was pointing as he looked down at his smart phone. When he looked up at Linus, there was a raw seriousness to his friend's face that he hadn't ever seen before. Linus had bare seconds to appreciate his friends and pack mates. They'd come through for him in ways that he'd never expected but would be eternally grateful for.

"Linus?" Jason asked, pulling him to a stop.

"This is the way I feel her, so maybe he took her there or maybe they passed by. It's worth a try."

Knowing there was at least something in the middle of the damn woods, he started at a jog and kept his wolf to the forefront of his brain. A half mile later, he felt a sudden shiver of fear lodge in his gut. Karly!

With a growl, he started to run at the exact moment that the scouts started to howl that they were on the trail of something. His friends, his pack, ran with him, Jason barking orders and preparing them for anything. He didn't want to think what Karly had suffered these hours she'd been gone. He was desperate to hold her. To see that she was okay.

They all stopped short in a clearing as they came upon the most shocking thing he'd ever seen. A man with white-blonde hair stood just outside a circle of wolves where Karly leaned against a tree holding her shoulder at an odd angle. These were no werewolves, they were real wolves. And from the looks of them, they were defending her!

An entire pack of over two dozen wolves circled her tightly, their faces towards the man that Linus knew was Phoenix. Growls seeped from their bared fangs that glistened like daggers in the bare moonlight. Jaws snapped with short, warning barks. More wolves came into the clearing, spilling out of the woods like they were being called to this place, the anger from the natural wolves as heavy on the air as Karly's fear.

Linus looked at Karly. "Baby?"

She slowly turned her gaze to him, and her face was wet with tears and her eyes were glossy with pain. She breathed his name, and it hitched in the middle, "Li-nus."

Phoenix spoke, "She's mine. I'll come back for her, and eventually I'll get her and disappear forever where you will never find us. You can't protect her forever." He took a step back, and something in his posture told Linus he was going to shift.

"She is my mate," Linus stepped forward through the ring of natural wolves towards Phoenix. "She is mine, and I will not let you have her. This ends tonight."

While they talked, the natural wolves had split into two groups and were now surrounding Phoenix and corralling him. They snapped at him like rabid beasts. His heart was racing so fast that his fear was a tangible thing on the air. His bravado slipped and fear shone through his features.

Behind the natural wolves, his pack mates who had shifted were watching, ready to stop him from leaving, and the rest of his pack in their human forms were standing by to help. Pride and courage flittered through him as he took another step forward. This was just one man. One pathetic excuse for a wolf had kidnapped an innocent woman over a childhood crush.

Linus' beast simmered under the surface. His human side wanted to go to Karly immediately, but his wolf wanted justice for its mate. He felt his eyes bleed to wolf amber as he let the beast loose further. Phoenix's eyes flashed as Linus lunged at him. He swiveled to bolt, but Linus' hands had gone to claws and they wrapped around his throat and slammed him to the ground before he could move or shift. Thick, black claws sprouted from Linus' fingertips and dug into the sides of Phoenix's neck. Blood welled around his claws as his human and wolf sides grew together in strength and rage. His fangs burst through his gums and his spine tickled in the way it would before he shifted, but it hovered there, beast and man combined.

"She. Is. Mine!" He howled, picking Phoenix up by the throat and slamming him back to the ground. Phoenix's hands clawed at his arms as his face turned from red to purple, and his claws dug further into his neck. His body thrashed underneath Linus', but merged with his beast as he was, Linus was too strong for Phoenix to overpower.

His human side wanted to break every bone in his body, one by one. His wolf wanted to spill his blood in the most violent way. This was not about revenge but about justice. And pack justice was swift and without suffering at the end. He would make Karly safe with Phoenix gone from their lives forever.

He let his beast take over further, and with a forceful twist, he snapped Phoenix's neck and ended the shadow he'd cast on his mate.

He stood up slowly, raised his head to the sky, and howled for the kill. His packmates – human and wolf – howled and the natural wolves joined in. Their chorus of a life taken for justice echoed through the woods. Stepping over the dead man's body, Linus met Karly's eyes. There was no fear there, no reproach for the violence she'd just seen, just love that shone brightly through her tears. He stumbled through the ring of wolves protecting her.

His claws and fangs receded with his beast and the knowledge that she was safe now. He knelt beside her, smoothing her hair from her face.

He scented over her and didn't smell blood, but from the way she was holding her shoulder, he could tell it was dislocated. "We need to get you to a hospital, baby. Do you think you can walk?"

She shook her head and made a gesture with her free hand towards her foot. Lifting the edge of her dirty jeans, he could see her ankle was swollen. "Okay, baby, I'm going to pick you up as carefully as I can."

He heard the sound of a truck coming near and knew that one of the wolves had gone back to get a vehicle so he didn't have to carry her far. She nodded and squeezed her eyes tightly shut when he slid his arms around her. As he stood, she whimpered through clenched teeth.

"We can burn him, like we did for the male that hurt Cades," Jason offered, as he turned around. They never said the name of that bastard that had kidnapped their alpha female. Phoenix's name would soon be remembered in the same way; a male that had hurt Linus' mate and died for it.

Michael walked over to them and made a gesture towards the body. "I don't think that will be necessary,"

The natural wolves gathered around the body and, with a coordinated snarl, began to rip him apart. His beast rumbled a growl of approval. That's what you do with crazy wolves who kidnap women. "Don't look, baby," he whispered and walked past the sight.

Bo was waiting with his pick up. Jason and Michael walked on either side of him. He'd never felt more blessed in his life than at that moment. His sweetheart was safe and his pack had supported him to the very end.

Michael said, "I'll drive your bike back to your house and pick up your truck and drive it to the hospital so you can use it if you need it."

"Thanks, Michael."

"I'll call your mom and grandparents, too. And let the rest of the pack know." Michael turned and jogged away. Jason opened the truck door for him.

"Brenda," Karly said with a rough voice, barely above a whisper.

"What about her?" Linus asked in surprise as he sat down in the truck and carefully positioned his mate on his lap.

"She's...she's in the cabin."

"What?" Jason asked in shock. "Brenda. Your ex-wife Brenda?"

Karly only nodded and took in a quiet slow breath and seemed to hover at the edge of unconsciousness.

"I'll handle it. You get your mate to the hospital and I'll check in with you later."

"Jason." Linus said. He turned back. "Thank you."

Jason nodded. "She's your mate, Linus. That means she's part of the pack and under the protection of all of us. I told you that one day I'd thank you for standing by me with Cades. It was my honor to help you bring her home."

Linus pulled the door carefully shut, and Jason slapped the hood and walked towards the cabin, barking orders for a few others to join him. Bo used his GPS to find the nearest hospital which was in Newport, twenty-five minutes away and texted the address to the pack so they could let his family know where they were going.

Karly was conscious but quiet, making little gasps of pain she tried to hide every time Bo pressed on the brakes or turned a corner or a bump appeared in the road. He wanted to ask her a thousand questions, but he kept them to himself and simply held her and whispered comforting things. That he loved her and was so sorry he had let her down.

It was nearly midnight when they got to the hospital. Karly had been away from him for over twelve hours. Frantic to know what had happened to her but afraid to push her too fast, he put her on a gurney in the emergency room that was set between other beds in a long line. No one was on either side of her, but the large emergency room was not empty by any stretch.

A handful of doctors and nurses came to check Karly over. She hadn't said a word since she mentioned Brenda, so Linus answered what questions he could. He told the story to the best of his ability while omitting a few truths. She'd been kidnapped by her deranged ex who had also kidnapped Brenda. Karly managed to escape and got injured. And the largest nod to the lie to keep them all safe was that when they found her, wolves had attacked her ex and killed him. The doctors asked why wolves would attack, and his suggestion was that it was some kind of protective instinct for them or that her ex had done something threatening to them.

With a rip of the curtain to cover the small area around the bed, Linus watched from the side as two nurses cut off her clothes and put her good arm through a gown to cover her, placing a light blanket across her legs. Her ankle was purple and swollen. She was taken to x-ray, and he took the opportunity to go out to make a call and found Jason in the waiting room.

When Jason told him that they had found Brenda severely beaten and chained up to a bed, Linus couldn't have been more shocked. Nearly hysterical with relief, Brenda had babbled the entire trip to the hospital about how sorry she was and what had happened.

"She's the one that contacted Phoenix. She apparently told him how to find Karly so that she could, you know, get her out of the way and get back with you," Jason said.

Linus' jaw dropped to the floor. "Are you fucking kidding me?"

Shaking his head, Jason pulled him out of the hospital and to the side of the building. "Michael asked her what she meant, and she told him that she wanted to get back together with you, so she used her friend at the police department to look Karly up. She saw her license plate on her little sports car. She knew there was a restraining order on Phoenix, but she sent him a letter anyway, saying that Karly was about to get married to a werewolf and wouldn't he like to come to town and put a stop to it. How the letter got to him from his last known address I don't know, but she told him where my house was and that Karly would be there on the full moon without much protection."

"Fuck."

"Yeah."

They stood in silence for several minutes. "I should, ah, go see if Karly's back from x-ray yet."

"She going to be okay?"

"Yeah. Her shoulder is dislocated, and something is wrong with her ankle. Nothing permanent."

"Good. I'll give your mom a call. They're on the way up here, and your bags are still in your truck, too. Do you have her parents' number? I can call them, too ,and give them an update."

"Thanks, man. For everything." He read off the number from his cell for her mother's phone, glad Jason was so on top of things.

Walking back to the where her bed had been, Linus waited in the empty area and thought over the shocking news. What had possessed Brenda to do something so dangerous and foolish? Had she so little concern for the life of another that she would willingly send an innocent woman back into the arms of her attacker? Even as he was glad that she hadn't gotten off scot-free, he was sorry that she'd been hurt.

The rhythmic creak of wheels echoed just before they brought her back into the room. The curtain was closed, and one doctor and one intern examined her shoulder. Linus was going to say her name and try to get a reaction out of her because she looked so lost and broken, but the doctor said, "This is going to hurt," and with the intern holding her, the doctor jerked her arm back into joint. She screamed in pain and passed out, and the young intern laid her gently back on the bed. Linus had to bite his cheek to keep from flashing his fangs and slaughtering the two men. It was hard to tell his beast that she'd needed to be hurt to be healed. He didn't much care for it himself.

Looking at him as the intern went to get a nurse, the doctor said, "That happens sometimes. She's going to be fine." The nurse came in with a sling, and Linus hovered while she put the gown on right and then attached the sling across her neck and positioned her arm in it before putting an IV in the top of her free hand.

"We're going to get some fluids into her. She's a little dehydrated, but we're also going to feed in some low dose pain medication and let her rest for the night. The ankle is bruised badly but not sprained or broken. They'll keep ice on her shoulder and ankle, and we'll give her a check in the morning and you should be able to take her home before lunch.

"She'll need to wear the sling for a while and do stretching exercises, and we'll keep her on anti-inflammatory and pain meds for a week or so. She may be back to normal in three or four weeks, but it could take up to three months before she's okay. I don't foresee any permanent damage or need for surgery, but she'll have a few follow up appointments with whoever her regular doctor is."

"Thanks." Linus extended his hand, and the doctor shook it. They moved her to a smaller room that had four beds in it, all of them blissfully empty. He took the current quiet to let his emotions go free, and he wept quietly by his mate's still form. He took little comfort in knowing she was safe forever now. The fact that she'd been so clearly traumatized and that he'd failed to keep her safe in the first place ate at him. After scrubbing his face with cold water in the small bathroom and getting his rolling emotions under control, he went to find his family.

His mother, grandmother, Tina, and Cadence cried when they saw her and hovered around her bed like the protective she-wolves they were. That Cadence had shown up surprised him in some ways but also spoke to the strength of her character and how much Karly had touched all of them in such a short amount of time. Cadence considered her a friend, and wolves looked out for their friends. Peter pulled them away from the women to the other side of the room and looked solemn.

He explained that Brenda was going to be staying overnight and that her friend had called her parents who were flying in to take care of her. The friend, Greta, had been fired as soon as Trick confirmed on the computer what files she had accessed. Brenda had been brutally raped for two days. Although her job had left messages at her house, no one had realized she had been kidnapped. Brenda told them that he was going to kill her by morning and that Karly had managed to get free of her bonds and escaped. She hadn't blamed her for leaving her behind, since it was her fault in the first place.

She apparently asked to see Karly and Linus to apologize in person, but Peter and Tina told her that they would extend her apologies for her and that they were certain that neither would want to see her. And they were right. Linus would have a hard time controlling his beast in the presence of the woman who had nearly cost him everything he loved.

The local police tried to contact the owner of the cabin and discovered he had passed away several years earlier and had no next of kin. They searched the cabin and found evidence of the kidnapping, which corroborated the story that Brenda told and what he had said. Brenda had not been witness to the natural wolves or what Linus had done and believed the story they had made up. They searched the immediate area but couldn't find a body. When they brought in dogs to try to find Phoenix, they had balked at the scent of the wolves and wouldn't search. Trick called Peter just minutes earlier to say the police in Newport were ruling him suspected of being dead by wolf attack and were closing the case.

Linus thanked Peter for his help, and the pack that was there, and joined his mother, grandmother, grandfather, Tina, and Cadence at Karly's bedside. "Do you think, uh, was she hurt very badly?" his mother asked him, looking about as small and unsure as he'd ever seen her. She clearly already thought of Karly as her daughter and seeing her unconscious in a hospital bed was hard for her, too.

"The nurse said that the only question she answered in x-ray was that she hadn't been touched." It wouldn't change the way he felt about her even if something had happened while she was gone, but he was glad that she wouldn't have memories of that nature.

His mother hugged her own mother and breathed out a thankful prayer. All night his family kept vigil with him, and so did Jason, Cadence, Peter and Tina. Michael showed up in the morning with breakfast for everyone, and brought in one of his and Karly's suitcases.

As his sweetheart started to wake up from the influence of the drugs, she blinked sleepy, drug-hazed eyes at him and reached for him with her free hand. "Oh, you look tired, Linus." She slurred.

"I'm good, baby," he kissed her fingers and blinked against the happy tears that threatened. "How do you feel?"

"Very nice." She smiled and wrinkled her nose.

Everyone laughed quietly, and she said in a loud whisper, "Why are they here?"

"Because they love you, too, baby."

Her brow arched in confusion. "Okay. I thought I was hurt or something." She drifted off to sleep again, and he let out a relieved breath as his family and friends chuckled over her drug-speak.

A few hours later, he was alone in the room with her, and she woke up for real, aware of her surroundings and in mild pain. After a meeting with the doctor and discharge instructions, he helped her dress in loose clothes and walked next to her as they wheeled her out of the hospital to his waiting truck. She was speaking, not as much as he would have liked, but at least she was talking. When she was safely buckled in and they started on the long drive home to Allen, he picked up her free hand and kissed it.

"Baby, I just wanted you to know that I'm so sorry I let you down. I'm sorry you were hurt because I failed. I keep misjudging my instincts and—"

"Just stop, okay? You already apologized like a hundred times." She was looking at him, and he met her eyes for a moment before having to watch the road again. "If there was anything to forgive, I would have forgiven you already. You couldn't watch me every second for the rest of our lives; it would have made us both insane. And if you'd tried to go into the bathroom with me, I would have thought you were off your rocker."

"I know, Karly, I just—"

"Stop, please. He didn't rape me. He didn't do anything except tie me to the headboard and feed me a peanut butter sandwich. I mean, he scared me shitless, but, Brenda is the one that got hurt. He was going to use a, uh, plain circular brand to melt off my tattoo and the mating marks. Then he was going to rape Brenda and kill her before he started our 'honeymoon'. The only thing I thought of when I tripped on that root and fell into the tree was that I wasn't going to get to say goodbye to you and tell you how much I loved you. I do love you. You came for me."

"I will always come for you, Karly. I love you more than anything in my life. It would have destroyed me if I'd lost you."

"But you didn't. So don't apologize anymore. You found me. You made things safe for us in the future. Phoenix is gone, and—" she broke off and started to cry. He pulled over as soon as he could and undid both their seatbelts, gingerly holding her while she wept.

"Thank you for saving my life, Linus," she whispered with a raw voice.

"You knew I would come for you, didn't you?" He pulled away and cupped her face with his hands, swiping his thumbs across her cheeks to catch the tears.

"I knew you wouldn't give up on me. How did you know where I was?"

"It was my wolf. I couldn't smell you, but I could feel you. I could sense your fear, and it was like a beacon for my beast. I let him loose enough to find you."

"Why did those real wolves protect me like that?"

"I'm not sure. When I talked to your mom this morning after you fell asleep again, she said that maybe because you're a supernatural creature linked to wolves that they felt the need to protect you. Whatever the reason, I'm glad they did. Their intervention gave me the time to get to you."

"Is Brenda going to be okay?"

He pressed a gentle kiss to her mouth. She was so tenderhearted and caring. "Physically, she'll be okay. Dehydrated, malnourished, and of course the physical abuse. Mentally, once she told everyone what had happened, she seemed to withdraw. Her family is coming for her, and they're going to take her back to Texas where she's originally from. I can't tell you how much it hurts me that my past almost took you from me."

"If you're not holding me responsible for Phoenix's behavior, then I can't hold you responsible for Brenda's. Our pasts almost destroyed us, but we survived. I just want to put this behind us and move forward."

"Me, too, love." He kissed her again as softly as he could.

He felt her smile against his mouth, and when he opened his eyes she said, "You get to play nurse to me for a few weeks, right?"

Little minx. "I'm at your service, baby."

She grinned devilishly, and he gave her a stern look and tried to tamp down the arousal that just seeing her feeling feisty again brought out. "You'll have to behave, young lady. That shoulder of yours is going to need lots of care. And I'm just the wolf to do it."

"Can I get you into a nurse's uniform maybe?"

He barked out a laugh, "Baby, I would wear anything to make you happy, but I draw the line at stockings and miniskirts." He momentarily flashed to seeing Michael in a French maid's uniform, complete with stockings and heels. It had taken him a long time before he could even look Michael in the eye after that.

"Aw, spoilsport."

Thinking it wise to get back on the road, they began their journey again, and after some careful adjustment and wincing, she settled against his shoulder and drifted off to sleep. Now that she was back with him, he felt like all was right with the world again. Those tense hours when he hadn't been able to find her had been a torturous hell he didn't wish to ever repeat.

He could let go of this time and love her the way she deserved. She was his sweet Angel Mate and he would spend the rest of his life loving her to the best of his ability.

# CHAPTER FIFTEEN

After a week of having Linus hovering over her and not letting her lift a finger for herself, she was more than ready to play. He took on the role of nurse very seriously, and although his mom and grandma both brought meals over for them and members of the pack stopped by daily, Linus was very strict about her being bothered. He was like a big muscular mother hen and she told him as much when he was showering with her last night so she "didn't strain herself" but refused to actually touch anything fun for more than a few swipes of the washcloth. "If you touch it more than three times, you're playing not cleaning," he told her in all seriousness, and she just stared up at him in shock.

She rolled her shoulder tentatively as she stared at her reflection in the bathroom mirror. She had two appointments that morning, one to a new OB for a checkup and to get her birth control shot, and one to the only doctor in town, who also happened to be a werewolf, to check out her shoulder. She really wanted him to tell Linus that she was cleared for sex. She didn't think she could handle being in bed with him one more night and not doing anything. She'd gone months before without having sex, but since she met Linus, she didn't want to play sex camel any longer than necessary.

After getting her birth control shot and being declared perfectly healthy from the waist down, they sat in the empty doctor's office and waited for her appointment. Tickling her fingers up the inside of his jean-covered thigh, he let her get about two inches away from his cock before he grabbed her hand and kept it still. "It doesn't matter what he says, baby, the doctor at the hospital said at least three weeks."

"Three weeks for strenuous shoulder-related activity, Linus." She felt like whining. "I'll go totally crazy if we don't make love soon, I mean it."

His blue eyes darkened slightly, and the muscle under one ticked. And that was it. "You'll live. I wouldn't risk hurting you if I got lost in the moment and grabbed you wrong. If you want me to take care of you when we get home, I will, but we won't be making love for at least two more weeks."

She swallowed the smart retort on her tongue and pulled her hand from his leg. Damn him and his sensible willpower!

As she expected but Linus didn't seem to care, the doctor – a very charming older man named Vincent Mirelli – said that she was cleared to resume some of her normal activities but nothing strenuous until after she came back in two more weeks for another check up. Her smug smirk was lost on Linus, so she decided to take matters into her own hands. Literally.

When they got home that Friday afternoon, Linus offered to make them an early dinner, and she just gave him a small, half smile and said, "I'll think about. I've got other things on my mind right now."

He smiled immediately but then scowled as if he remembered what he'd said. "I haven't changed my mind, love."

"I didn't ask you to. In fact, I don't think I remember inviting you, anyway." She tapped her finger to her chin thoughtfully and then walked away to the bedroom. She was not a girl without options. If he wasn't going to give her what she wanted or do it only half way, then she was going to take care of herself. Period.

She wasn't ashamed of her vibrator but hadn't had an occasion to bring it out, and Linus never asked if she had one. She opened her seldom-used second travel bag and pulled out the velvet drawstring pouch that contained her toy.

She tossed it to the bed and began to strip. "Just what the hell are you doing?" He demanded, looking between her and the black bag.

"I'm taking care of myself."

"I said I'd help you, Karly." He frowned.

She shook her head, determination giving her a little courage. "No thanks."

He looked completely stunned. "You don't want me to touch you?"

"No, I don't want you to touch me halfway. I need to feel you inside me, Linus, and just your fingers or just your mouth…it's not enough. I'd rather play alone and try to take the edge off this uncontrollable lust I'm feeling right now than not really be satisfied."

When she climbed on the bed and pulled the toy from the bag he growled and snatched it from her hand. "Hey!" she yelled.

"You are out of your mind if you think I'm going to compete with an electronic toy. Nobody brings you pleasure but me. You're mine, Karly." His eyes were dark and feral, just the edge of his control coming loose like a flag in the wind.

"Either fuck me yourself or get out and leave the toy."

"I think…you're not in control here, Karly." His mouth quirked up in the corner, and her breath caught. "Now, prop yourself up on pillows so your shoulder doesn't have any pressure on it and spread your legs."

Adjusting the pillows against the headboard, she settled up into a nearly upright position and spread her legs, bending her knees slightly and planting her heels.

"Naughty girl," he narrowed his eyes, putting her toy down and pulling his shirt off. "Look at how wet you are already."

Her toes curled into the comforter, and her temperature went up about twenty degrees. He dropped his pants to the floor, and her mouth watered at the sight of him, hard and ready. It felt like a hundred years since she'd seen him naked with a look of want and hunger in his eyes.

He climbed up between her legs and sat back on his heels, looking at her vibrator and then at her. He clicked the button on the bottom after inspecting it and began to draw slow, swirling lines up the inside of her leg, starting at the top of her foot. On low, it tickled and felt good. When he reached her knee, he pushed the button again, and it clicked up to medium speed. Rounding the top of her thigh, he switched legs, drawing lazy patterns all around her calf and the inside of her knee, switching to the highest setting.

Now this was torture. Hot, sexy, lovely torture with the man that was going to be her husband. He drew closer and closer with each pass to her tingling core but never stopped until he'd covered everything with little patterns but the one place she wanted him to touch.

Gritting her teeth with another unsuccessful pass by her pussy, he chuckled. "Aw, am I doing this wrong, baby?"

"You know exactly what you're doing," she bit out.

"True. I just wondered how long it would take you to actually say something." He leaned up and kissed her, slanting his mouth to hers and pushing his tongue to slide against hers. Tangling her fingers in his hair, she kissed him back and forgot he had a humming little pleasure toy in his hands until he pushed it inside her suddenly and she came to blistering awareness on the crest of a powerful climax. She twisted her fingers in his hair as she cried out in pleasure. He pressed his forehead to hers while the pleasure danced freely up and down her body.

He experimented with the vibrator, pulsing it inside her weeping body in varying speeds and angles until her thighs trembled with tension and her heart attempted to pound out of her chest.

"Time for the real thing, baby," he kissed her once and moved away, stretching out on his back across the bed. She practically launched herself at him, and he chuckled while she adjusted herself to straddle him and take him inside. Wasting no time at all, she threw her body down onto his until they were as close as possible and she cried out with the fullness of him. She could have cried real tears of joy for making love again, but something wet and vibrating on high speed pressed into her clit and she nearly rocketed off him.

One hand gripped her thigh, and the other held the vibrator against her swollen nub. With growled words, he encouraged her to ride him as hard as she wanted, to take what belonged to her. She could not have stopped if the world was crashing down around them. She found a rhythm that called to a deep part of her, closing her eyes to everything except the feelings and sounds between them. So deep together, it was as if they were one person now, her body humming with the vibrations against her clit and his cock filling her so perfectly. When a second orgasm from the toy on her clit pounded down on her, he tossed the vibrator aside and grasped her hips, pushing her down onto his body while his hips thrust up in wild rhythm.

"Ah, Linus!" she screamed, digging her nails into his wrists and twisting on him as her body tried to split apart and liquid heat spilled from her.

He came right after her, "Fuck, Karly!"

She slipped carefully to his chest, gasping for breath and slick with sweat. A shiver wove through him, and he kissed her forehead. "You're okay, baby?"

"I'm wonderful, Linus, thank you."

"Well, I couldn't have you falling in love with a toy that has unbelievable staying power."

She laughed and sighed. "Nothing's better than your cock, Linus, and that's the truth."

"Good to know," he chuckled.

"I love you, Linus."

"I love you, too, Karly"

With the danger of her past erased except from memory, they decided to go back to their original plan of going to her parents' pack before the March full moon and having the Angel ceremony as well as the full moon hunt. Linus' family was coming, but because it was a full moon, Linus decided not to ask any of his friends to join them. He reasoned that they could enjoy a full moon hunt with her family on the full moon for their pack joining and Angel ceremony for the Tressel Pack, and he wanted to enjoy their time together with her parents with the two families coming together.

Linus spent a lot of time with Pops and Alpha Jason's grandfather Abraham, talking about the "old ways" and what the pack used to be like. She knew he was worried about being deficient in some way to Alpha Krayne or her father, and she wanted him to ease his own mind. Her father understood that Linus had not been raised in a pack like theirs, and without his father as a strong influence on him, he was like that last leaf on a branch in fall, left to fend for itself.

The night before their trip, after they made love and were tangled together in her favorite way, he broke the silence of the dark bedroom. "I wanted to tell you about my father and his family."

She tried to move, to sit up and look at him, but he locked his arms around her and said with a rough voice, "It will be easier, baby, if you don't look at me right now, okay?"

"Okay." She settled back to where she was splayed across half his body, her head against his shoulder and her arm and leg spread across him.

"Jack Mayfield got my mom pregnant and married her out of obligation. He didn't want to be married or have a child so he began to drink and whore around town, or really, he never stopped doing it even after he got married. He would come home smelling like perfume and whiskey. He didn't bother to hide it. When I was eight, I was playing in their room, and I saw the edge of a picture sticking out from the drawer, one of those Kodak pictures. I pulled it out and turned it over, and it was the girl that babysat me and she was naked. I didn't understand why there was a naked picture of her in my father's drawer, so I took it to my mom and she freaked out. I was in bed when he got home that night and she confronted him, and then the yelling started. I crept from my room in time to see him slam her against the wall and tell her to stay out of his things. I cried and ran to her, and he kicked me like a dog, and told me I was the worst thing that ever happened to him."

He stopped talking for a long moment, and she blinked back the tears that threatened.

"Once he hit her that first time, he started to hit her all the time, and when I would try to protect her, then I was in the crosshairs, too. She tried to protect me, but he was a big man — not muscular, just big — and he just hit her all the more when she stood up for me. She hid the abuse from everyone. Then one night I went to stay at my grandma's house, and she walked into the bathroom when I was getting out of the shower and saw the bruises on my back. Pops went over there with some of the other men in the pack, but he was already gone. He'd grabbed that underage babysitter he'd taken the picture of and ran off. Maybe he knew it was just a matter of time before his behavior became pack knowledge, or maybe he just got tired of the pretense of being married, I don't know. But he was gone, and he never contacted us again. His parents were part of our pack. They never wanted anything to do with me or my mom. They thought we were beneath them, just so much trash. It wasn't too long after my father left that they left the pack and went out west somewhere." His fingers traced invisible patterns on her back in the silence that followed. She waited for him to say more or not but to let her know either way, and eventually he did.

"I worry sometimes about being a father, because I don't have a very good image in my mind of what a father should be like, but Pops reminded me a few days ago that I did have that all around me. In the men in the pack that looked out for us. And the men in my mom's family are all the examples that I ever needed. All the stuff that I've been learning about the history of our kind has just made me all the more determined to raise our children right. To give them that sense of belonging and family that comes with being a werewolf but also to teach them the weight that such a special family carries. If my father had been a better man and wolf, he would have just walked away and left us be, but something kept him around long enough to torment us." He tipped her chin up so she could see him.

"I just needed you to know about some of the things that haunt me. I know you're smart enough to have figured out that I have issues with my father, and before we make the commitments to each other with your parents' pack, I wanted you to know what creeps around in the dark parts of my mind."

She kissed him tenderly and thanked him softly for telling her about his demons, and they made love once more and chased the darkness away from both of them before coming down from the heavens to sleep.

# CHAPTER SIXTEEN

Linus couldn't believe what the Soualit Pack was really like. It was like a small city that revolved around the alpha, a man his grandfather's age who looked like he could take on anyone, anytime and win. He wasn't a big man, but lean and muscular with a face that was wrinkled, but not from smiling too much. His hair had been dark once but was mostly gray now, and his wife was a small woman with short curly white hair and soft blue eyes.

Karly was hands down the most beautiful woman he'd ever laid eyes on. And it was very clear where she got her beauty from. Her parents were almost too beautiful for words, like living pieces of art, and her brothers were just about the most handsome men he'd ever seen, although he'd never admit it out loud. Karly's mother Sophia looked like a porcelain doll, with ivory skin and dark hair. Her father Kamren was very tall and well built, with olive skin and thick black hair cut short. Her three brothers were just younger versions of their father, all with the same olive skin and black hair. Bren, Rico and Graise gave him a good once over and then grinned and slapped him on the back in what he assumed was a brotherly sort of thing. Since he had no experience with siblings, he would have to just take their lead.

Sophia and his mom and grandma dove right into getting things ready for the ceremony at dawn, and he felt Karly's fingers slipping from his hand as she was pulled away from him.

"Don't worry, son," Kamren said, "you'll see her at dinner. You know women." Linus' grandfather was invited to visit with the alpha, so he left Linus with his future in-laws.

"Hades," Bren frowned as they walked together towards her parents' house, "when Kelina gets wind of this ceremony, she's going to want me to drape her in fucking expensive orange blossoms, too!" Kelina was Bren's wife, and they were alpha-mates of a pack in Ontario.

Bren said to him, "My wife's up in my folks' house with the babies. She just had our third over Christmas, so she's kind of, you know, busy."

"Congratulations," he offered.

"Well, you're their uncle now. Add Angel, instant family."

Graise snorted, "You're so damned lucky. Ma said it's like love at first sight. You didn't have to fend off a whole pack full of wolves to claim her."

Rico laughed, "You're just mad because you almost lost your wife to that stock broker!"

Without warning, Graise launched himself at Rico, and they went tumbling to the grass, throwing playful punches and calling each other names. Rico managed to get to his feet, but Graise grabbed his pants leg and he tripped and went down and Rico cursed and flipped to all fours and pounced on Graise.

"They're such idiots." Bren laughed as they stopped to watch the show.

"Yes, they are. But they're your brothers, so you're stuck with them," Kamren said.

"And now you are too, brother." Bren looked at Linus and gave him a sincere smile.

He marveled at the sense of family that surrounded him so easily here. Bren was the oldest at thirty-two, Rico was twenty-nine, Graise was twenty-five. They were all married to she-wolves, alphas of their packs, and all had children. And what was even more amazing was that they just accepted him right into the fold like they'd known him for years.

Inside the huge home that was more like a boarding house than anything, the first thing Linus saw was a tall blonde woman cradling a baby in her arms and rocking it back and forth while it wailed. "Oh, good!" She smiled tightly, "Your son wants his father."

"How come when he's crying he's my son?" Bren groused good-naturedly, crossing the room to kiss his wife on the cheek and take the squalling child from her arms.

After introductions were made first to Kelina, Bren's wife, and then Lorna, Rico's wife, and then Katie, Graise's wife, Bren handed the still crying child to Linus. "Here's your nephew Kellan. Get him to calm down, would ya?"

Linus stared down at the red-faced baby in half alarm and did the only thing he could think of. He put the baby over his shoulder and patted him on the back like he'd seen the she-wolves in the pack do. After a few good pats, little Kellan burped loud enough to wake the dead and then quieted down with a happy sigh.

"Aw, Uncle Linus has the golden touch. Quick, go grab Metz!" Graise grinned, speaking about his own young son.

As the day progressed and the pack welcomed them as visitors and soon to be relatives, they prepared for the full moon by way of a large sit down meal at the alpha's home. The dining room table easily held twenty, and another table set up in a connected room held another ten. Adults-only, the children were spirited away by she-wolves in the pack so the parents could enjoy the meal.

Alpha Krayne and his mate Mary presided over the elaborate meal that

Karly had helped her mother and the three other caretakers make, consisting of different kinds of roasted meats, large bowls of side dishes, and a side table full of desserts. Joining the alpha pair, Karly's family, and Linus' own, the table was full and inviting, just like the picture Karly had painted for him. After the Alpha said a prayer of thanks over the meal, everyone dug in, plates were passed and meat was carved into huge wedges for the hungry wolves.

When dinner was over, Karly pulled him away from the table after assuring her father they would return in less than an hour to prepare for the full moon hunt. Once outside on the porch, she gave him a crooked smile and took off, racing towards her parents' home. She was fast, but Linus was faster, and although he let her win, he was just a step behind her and swung her up into his arms to carry her through the door and into the empty house.

"You let me win," she murmured against his mouth, wriggling in his arms.

"Prove it."

"You're not even breathing hard."

Busted. Chuckling, he set her down and said, "We only have an hour."

"I know. But I missed you today, and I wanted to just sit and talk for a bit. You're going to be gone all night, and then we'll have the ceremony and the party that lasts all day. We won't get to be alone again until tomorrow night when the sun sets."

It was going to be a very long night and day. "Good thing there will be coffee."

They sat together on a comfortable leather sofa in the front room. After a long, gentle kiss, she said, "What do you think of everything you've seen so far?"

Where to start? "Karly, I love it here. I can see why you hold this way of life in such high regard. The sense of belonging and family is just amazing. And your parents, hell your whole family, is just incredible."

"My brothers are so excited to have some new blood in the family. I wish we had more time to spend here so you could get to know them better, but being away from their packs at the full moon is hard for them. In the summer, they've always come here for a few weeks. We could join them, if you'd like." Her fingers slid through the hair over his ears slowly, a warm smile on her face, her eyes shining with happiness.

He pulled her into his arms. "I'd love that. I want our family to be a haven for our children, the way that you feel here — I want to have that back in Allen. Will you help me, love?"

"Of course, my sweet wolf," she sighed, rubbing her cheek against his. "I'm going to miss you while you go hunting."

"I'll catch you something big, okay?"

Grinning, she tipped her face up for another kiss, and he willingly obliged until the time slipped away all too fast and they were on their way to the pack's full moon meeting place.

The Tressel Pack had less than forty adult members. The Soualit Pack had twenty-one members. When Karly said small, she meant it. But somehow, standing next to his mate in front of the small pack as they curved in a circle around the blazing bonfire, he felt like he was in the presence of a pack that would go marching into hell for one of their own and never think twice. It wasn't the camaraderie of friends the way that the Tressel Pack was, it was more of a large family led by a father figure in the alpha who would never let his people down. It was similar in kind but different in way of life. He wasn't really sure which was better, except that he wanted his and Karly's children to know both worlds and then make their own way.

The pack consisting of eight females including Karly's mother and thirteen males watched the alpha intently as if everything he spoke was liquid gold. With a booming voice, he said, "The moon spirit beckons us this night, to pay homage to our kindred that have gone on before us, remembering the ways of our past and our lineage. The taking of life is as sacred as the creation of it, and we do so tonight as we do each full moon, in full thanks for the animals that will give their lives in sacrifice to our pack.

"It is a great honor to extend our hunt tonight to include Linus Mayfield and his grandfather Eugene Jackson in our hunt. Linus is the chosen mate of Kamren's daughter, Karolyn. This hunt is for their pack welcome tonight. We hunt with them in mind.

"Forget not the claw that does harm tonight, that it should do good tomorrow for the sake of our souls. Cast your mantel from your body and show your true form!"

With a howl like something out of a horror film, the Alpha shouted to the moon, stripped and shifted in a blink to reveal an enormous black wolf, much larger than any Linus had seen before. Karly smiled at him, and he pulled his jeans off and shifted. She came close to him, gathering his things from the ground, and he nuzzled her cheek and licked her jaw before darting off after the rest of the pack, his grandfather hot on his tail, ignoring the arthritic aches in his joints for the night.

Hunting with the pack was incredible. The terrain was rocky and rough, the trees so thick that there was barely space to get between them, but his instincts were so finely tuned that it felt like he'd been part of the pack his whole life. Karly's brothers were dark gray like Kamren, and they all hunted together, racing towards a herd of deer that had been drinking from a partially frozen stream.

With his heart pounding in his ears and a few millennia of wolf instinct coursing through his veins, he barreled through the herd towards one of the bucks, the moonlight highlighting the curve of horns just seconds before it took off. Linus was faster than its attempt to get away, snagging it on the haunches with his claws and tumbling it to the ground. As he'd done for as long as he hunted, he snapped his jaws around the writhing beast's neck and choked the breath from its lungs. As the creature gave up and its life slipped away, Linus disengaged from his kill and would have had a big grin on his face if he'd been human. It felt good to kill quickly, to know his instincts were right where they should be. For a mated wolf, it meant that the whole pack would have no doubt that he could take care of his mate.

Wolves appeared around him, including Pops, and helped him begin the long trek back dragging his prize. The woods were filled with dragging sounds and grunts of exertion as others including Kamren, Alpha Krayne, and one of Karly's brothers, dragged a buck, and her two other brothers had a black bear between them.

By the time they made it back to the lunar meeting place with their kills, enough time had passed that they were all able to shift back to their human forms. Dawn was three hours away. The caretakers appeared and began to butcher the kills along with most of the males.

Linus didn't know how to butcher anything, and fortunately, it wasn't his job. "Come, son," Kamren said, gesturing for him to follow, "you've got some things to do to prepare to take your Angel."

They walked back to their home, Kamren, his three sons, and Pops, and Kamren sent him off to shower and dress in the clothes that had been laid out for him in one of the guest bedrooms. The room was small and tidy, with a full-size bed covered in a blue quilt and matching curtains on the window.

Linus showered, still exhilarated with the hunt. He'd not taken down a buck in a long time. Their pack hunted in groups of three or four. This was the first hunt he'd been on since he turned at sixteen that he hadn't been with Jason, Michael and Bo. It had been strange to hunt with Karly's family but also familiar in a way he hadn't expected.

Drying his hair, he dressed in the clothes laid out for him, what he assumed was traditional for the Angel ceremony. Hand stitched buckskin trousers hung low on his hips, with a matching embroidered vest. On the front of the vest, Karly's tattoo was stitched with shiny black and gold thread.

Opening the bedroom door, he walked down to the front room where Kamren, Pops, and his three brothers-in-law were wearing identical clothes, minus the embroidered tattoo on the vest.

He noticed none of them had shoes on either, so he didn't mention the lack of them. "Did Karly explain the ceremony?" Kamren asked.

"Kind of."

"Well, it's pretty straight forward. My wife will officiate over the angel part and then alpha Krayne will welcome you into the pack as the mate of a member, which gives you the status of honored guest for the span of your life. Then the pack will walk by you single file and they'll embrace you one by one. It's a way to cement your scent into their memory as well as welcome you. When that's done, you'll be presented with the gifts from the pack in the form of the hides of the kills. The meat will be cooked, and you'll have a chance to rest before the evening meal, but you'll have to rest alone and without Karly. After the meal, you'll have to stick with the party until sunset, and then you'll come back here and stay in our home for the night. Sophia has made up the largest guest room for you to make yourself comfortable. In the morning, there will be a large breakfast at the alpha's, and then you can head home afterwards."

They began to walk out towards the full moon meeting place. "You could always join this pack, you know." Rico said, falling into step next to him. "If you wanted, I mean. We all have our own packs and all, but your Pops was telling us how modern your pack is. Alpha Krayne would welcome you and Karly as full members."

Linus was a little speechless. It had crossed his mind because Karly was so happy to be home with her family, but he had responsibilities to his own pack, not to mention his own family.

"Now, now, don't rush the boy," Kamren chided his son. "There's time for life altering decisions another day."

Glad he didn't have to say one way or the other what he thought, he kept his mouth shut and followed them to the open space and tried not to think about how frozen his feet were getting already.

The sky was the most possible black it could be just before sunrise as he stood alone in the center of the full moon meeting place. The bonfire had been extinguished, and all the wolves around him were quiet in anticipation. A torch dotted the darkness, drawing closer, Karly's mother's face shining in the play of light and shadow.

He could just barely make out Karly walking behind her mother through the trees and into the sacred circle. Sophia dipped the flaming end of the torch into the bonfire, and it roared to life, laid heavy with new wood soaked with an accelerant to burn quickly. She placed the torch in a tall holder next to a small wooden stand with a book on it.

As Karly drew close to him, Linus was simply stunned. She looked like a vision. A real angel. Wearing a plain white long gown, her shoulders were draped with a cloak made of pure white rabbit pelts that trailed the ground. She reached her hands out for his, and he took them, finding hers trembling and ice cold. Immediately he wanted to pull her into his arms and warm her up, but he fought the urge and tried reasoning with his wolf that this was tradition and important.

Sophia wore a similar gown of plain white, but her cloak was gray, like fox fur. In her hands, she held a length of green vine full of white flowers that smelled like oranges. With quiet care, she wrapped the two of them up in the vine, threading it across his shoulders and down both arms and their clasped hands and tied it around Karly's shoulders. The whole time, he was only barely aware of anything except the sweet, love-filled look on Karly's face as the sun began to rise and cast the woods in amber light.

Sophia stood behind the small stand and opened the book. Clearing her throat, she looked up at the sky and then at the two of them.

"When the first wolf was created, too full of his beast to be man, the great wolf spirit felt pity for him and his misery and sent him an angel. She was his salvation; a perfectly made mate for his beast and his human natures twined together in one being. The Angel Mate was created on that day so the werewolf would not have to choose between his beast nature and his human nature. Because of the Angel Mate, the werewolf could live in society as he was meant to: a protector of innocents, a leader of his kind, a father to his pups, and most importantly, mate to his angel.

"We celebrate the joining of the last Angel Mate to her wolf this morning, as the sun rises on this first new day of their life together. May the wolf spirit and the spirit of the first Angel shine down on you for the span of your lives and bless you with pups and angels to fill your home with love." Sophia paused for just a moment, tears shining in her eyes, and as the sun broke through the horizon and rose silently in the sky, she said with a loud, clear voice, "Fentrita Kil-arne Postur. May the love you share between you keep you warm for all eternity. Angel, Wolf, Family."

Without a signal, the wolves in the pack lifted their heads to the sky and howled. "What has been joined together this day," Sophia said as she undid the vine of orange blossoms from around them, "let none destroy." Plucking two blossoms from the vine, she tucked one behind Karly's left ear and put the other in a small stitched loop in his vest and then turned to the fire and cast the entire length into it. With a cheer, the wolves clapped and shouted their approval, and Sophia turned with a smile and said, "You can kiss your mate now, son."

Not wasting a second, he pulled Karly into his arms and claimed her mouth, feeling as if it had been weeks since he'd enjoyed the sweet, hot taste of her. When the ruckus from the wolves died down, they pulled apart, and his family and hers were standing around them.

"It's time for the pack to join you, son," Kamren said, "and then we'll take you back to our home for the day to rest."

His family and hers hugged both of them, his mom and grandmother with tears in their eyes and his grandfather looking as proud as he'd ever seen him. Alpha Krayne welcomed him as an honored guest of the pack for the span of his life and, in a move that surprised him, hugged him and clapped him on the back. Nodding but saying nothing, Linus held Karly's hand tightly as the pack filed by, including his new brothers-in-law and their wives. Congratulations were offered, but all Linus could think was that he'd have to spend the day without her. They hadn't been apart this much since her abduction, and it gnawed at his beast. He tried to hide his displeasure, but the moment the last of the wolves had hugged them both and committed his scent to memory, he had to let go of her hand and it felt like a part of him was being left behind.

Kamren, Pops, and Karly's brothers surrounded him and began walking, and after glancing back and seeing her being led away as well, he frowned and tried to concentrate on what his new father-in-law was saying but it was difficult. He missed her. He needed her. Damn traditions!

Back at Kamren and Sophia's house, Kamren stopped at the bottom of the stairs. "You can change out of your ceremonial clothes. You'll want to keep those for your future son-in-law the way that I did for you. For the party tonight, you can wear whatever you like. It would be a good idea to get some rest, even though we all know how hard it is to be separated from your mate. Welcome to the family, son. You've made my little girl very happy."

Linus trudged up the stairs feeling like his feet were now blocks of ice from being shoeless. Exhaustion plucked at him, but he wanted nothing more than to run out and find Karly and drag her into his arms and finish that kiss.

Too keyed up to sleep, he opted to take a nice, hot shower until his body unfroze. Drying off, he looked at the clothes he'd folded carefully on the counter. He was surprised to know that Kamren had worn them. Once more, he was overwhelmed by tradition. He wanted very badly to be able to pass on all the knowledge he was surrounded by at this moment. Taking a deep breath of the orange blossom and thinking of his mate, he walked out into the bedroom and realized immediately he wasn't alone.

Karly, still wearing her white dress but minus the cloak, was sitting in the middle of the bed. He paused and then climbed hurriedly onto the bed, the towel around his waist disappearing with his haste.

She laughed quietly as he covered her face with kisses and held her close. "You have to leave, don't you? Don't go, baby, please." He whispered, "I can't bear another second away from you."

"I snuck out." She wiggled her brows at him. "We shouldn't make love, but we can sleep together. I miss you, too."

"I'll be good, I swear." He nodded vigorously. At that point, he would have agreed to being bound hand and foot to the bed just to have her there.

"Then put something on, please, so I'm not so tempted." She made an exaggerated motion of covering her eyes, and he glanced down to see his cock hadn't really wanted her to go anywhere, either.

"Right." He darted off the bed and rummaged in the suitcase.

"Toss me a shirt and some panties, would you?" She asked, and he heard the sound of a zipper and just barely stopped himself from turning around and ravaging her. With a flick, he tossed a pajama top and panties behind him and pulled on briefs. When he heard the covers being moved, he felt it was safe to turn around.

She had adjusted the blinds and drapes so that the room was bathed with only a bare glow of early morning sunlight. Patting the pillow next to her, she smiled at him invitingly, and he didn't have to be asked twice.

"So will we get in trouble?" He teased her as he pulled her sweet, heavenly body against his.

"Nah. My mom snuck out to be with my dad, too. And besides, the point of the separation was so that the Angel's family could prepare her to leave if she needed to, pack her things, and also prepare her for the wedding night. I imagine that a few generations ago, Angels weren't making love to their mates ahead of the joining ceremony and would have wanted the counsel of their elders."

"I'm so happy you're mine, Karly. I couldn't live without you."

She tipped her face to his, her eyes happy but sleepy. "I love you, Linus. My sweet wolf."

With a long, soft kiss, they said goodnight, and he cuddled her against his chest while both he and his wolf sighed in contentment and drifted off to sleep.

Later that night, they gathered with the Soualit Pack for the equivalent of a wedding reception, rustic-wolf-style. Rough-hewn picnic tables were laden with platters of food. Spits of wedges of different game caught from their hunt were roasting over an enormous bonfire.

Alpha Krayne and Mary were standing in front of the fire when Kamren, Rico, Graise, Bren, Linus and Pops walked into the clearing and joined them.

The pack joined them in a loose circle. Through an opening, Sophia led Karly, his mother and grandmother into the clearing. His mate looked so beautiful he could hardly keep his feet rooted to the ground.

She wore a white long-sleeved sweater and a long skirt. Her hair was fixed up at the sides with the orange blossom tucked behind her ear. His sweetest angel.

Alpha Krayne took Karly's hand and kissed her cheek. "When two among our kind find their truemates, it is cause for great celebration. Let us join in celebration tonight for Linus and Karly."

Linus took Karly's hand and pulled her into his arms once more as his wolf rumbled his approval with the first, but not the last, kiss of the night. The pack clapped and cheered until the kiss broke. Within minutes, they were seated and enjoying the fruits of the hunt.

Over the years, he had eaten his share of game, but the Tressel Pack didn't bring the kills back and slaughter and then cook them. It was very traditional and ensured that nothing was wasted. And it also meant that Karly was taking a bite of the buck he'd killed. There was something very thrilling about that. In the most primal of ways, he was providing for his mate. He made a mental note to talk to Jason about it once they were back in Allen.

"Penny for your thoughts?" Karly whispered in his ear.

He put his fork down and put his arms around her, kissing her ear and nuzzling the warm spot just behind it. "I'm going to give you about five minutes to finish eating."

"Oh?" She laughed softly. "You can wait that long?"

It was his turn to laugh. "I was just being polite."

She peeked up at him and grinned. "We can always be polite over breakfast."

Excellent point. Although his wolf would have liked to haul her over his shoulder like a caveman and race off to plunder her sweet body, his human side knew the better, less offensive thing to do was to say goodnight to everyone.

When the pleasantries were done, they walked hand in hand away from the celebration towards her parents' house. His mind raced as they drew closer to the house. This seemed like the sort of night that should burn in your memory forever.

As her hand reached for the door, he swung her up into his arms and pushed it open, carrying her across the threshold and kicking it shut. She fisted her hands in his hair and attacked his neck, and he barely made it into the guest bedroom without plowing them into the wall for her expert distraction.

Leaning heavily on the closed door, he looked around the room taking quick stock. Their bags were on the dresser. The bed had been turned down. Candles waited to be lit. A platter of cut fruit sat on a small table with a bottle of wine in an ice bucket and two glasses. Putting Karly down on the floor, he kissed her and then went to light the candles.

"Was this your room, baby?" He asked, tipping a tall, fat candle sideways to catch the wick.

"No. My dad turned my room into a den. This was Rico's room."

He lit the candles and opened the wine, pouring half glasses for both of them before flicking off the overhead light. "I am the luckiest man on the planet, and I've been that way since I found you. My sweet little snow angel." He tipped his glass to hers in a quiet toast, and they both took a drink. He really didn't want anything to get in the way of remembering all that they were going to do tonight, so he took the glass from her hand and put both of them back.

"Later," he said, reaching for her hands and clasping them in his.

Her smile was the one he loved so much. The kitten and the wildcat mixed up together. "Do me a favor, baby?"

"Anything."

"Strip for me."

He left her standing and sat down in a plush armchair near the window. She started immediately, kicking off her shoes. As she unzipped the long skirt, he grinned at his good fortune. His sweetheart really was perfect for him. She had almost zero inhibitions, she was as sweet as she was stunning, and she loved him. What more could a man ask for?

Their night passed in a blur of tangled limbs, panting cries of pleasure, and one broken lamp thanks to a stray foot. After breakfast, they headed back home to Allen. Once more he was very aware that he felt like he was part of a larger family now. Not just a wolf family, but a human family. Karly's parents and brothers and sisters-in-law had stepped right up and accepted him without reservation. Having Karly was the best thing, but having her family's support in addition to his own was icing on a perfect cake. He'd never been happier in his life.

# CHAPTER SEVENTEEN

"It's my great pleasure, as Alpha of the Tressel Pack, to welcome the mate of one of our wolves to our pack as a treasured member and to announce for the first time anywhere, Mr. and Mrs. Linus Mayfield!" Jason said loudly, as Linus and Karly turned from where he had officiated the pack joining ceremony just minutes after the Angel ceremony and their legal marriage ceremony performed by a justice of the peace in the full moon meeting place back in Allen. June 30th would forever be the very best day of her life, when all the pieces of the puzzle of her life came together just perfectly.

Her mom and Linus' mom, already thick as thieves, cried together, and Linus' grandmother beamed at the two of them. Even her dad and Pops looked like they were struggling to contain their happiness and it was very easy to see that Linus was trying to hold his own emotions in check. Men could be so silly sometimes.

They walked through the makeshift aisle between the wolves, and the ones lining the edge showered them with rose petals as they walked from the full moon meeting place back to Jason and Cadence's home where the reception was being held. Her father had offered to throw them a big wedding, but in all honesty, neither Linus nor she really wanted anything like that. They just wanted to share their day with the people that meant the most to them, and that included her brothers and their families, Alpha Krayne and Mary, Linus' family, and the Tressel Pack.

Long tables and chairs had been set up outside in the clearing behind Jason and Cadence's home, several mounded with food that her mother and sisters-in-law had been up all night preparing. It had been the last night without Linus that she hoped would ever happen. It seemed silly to keep that tradition, since they'd been living together for several months, but everyone kept talking about jinxing happiness and breaking long-standing traditions, so they gave up arguing. She stayed at Linus' mother's house and he stayed at their house with Jason, Michael and Bo and had the wolf version of a bachelor's party: shifting and hunting.

The hides that her parents' pack had given them for their joining ceremony had been given to a tailor who made two matching suede jackets for Linus and her, a long swing skirt for her, and two decorative pillows. And they had enough deer meat in their freezer to last until they were old and gray. Not to mention all that they'd divvied up between the two packs.

Her dress was a simple strapless a-line, with lace and beading on the bodice. Her hair was pulled up and twisted around diamond clips that belonged to her father's mother. Linus sent a gift to her in the morning of a beautiful diamond pendant. They'd decided that, instead of getting a separate engagement ring and using his family ring as the wedding band that he could buy her a wedding band instead, because she loved the band that he had given her when he proposed and she didn't want anything else to be substituted. The ring he picked out for her was a gorgeous eternity band that sparkled on her finger like it was covered with tiny little stars. His own band was plain platinum that she'd had inscribed with their names.

After Jason toasted them as best man and then joined them at the head table, they ate their fill at dinner and then danced on a makeshift dance floor while the DJ from the bar played their song.

It was just absolutely a perfect day. As the sun began to set and the suggestion was made to move the party to the bar – without them – so they could continue to have fun, her parents came to see them.

They'd been waiting to know what they were going to give them. They'd promised to send Karly and Linus somewhere on their honeymoon and had only told them to pack for the beach, but otherwise they had no clue.

She opened the dark red envelope and pulled out two first class tickets to Newport, Rhode Island along with their itinerary and a black credit card with both their names on it. She gaped at her father.

"I know how much you loved visiting the ocean as a child, so we're giving you a week in Newport, all expenses paid. Your hotel and towncar are paid for, and everything else should be put on the card. Take lots of pictures, darling. And have a wonderful honeymoon." Her father kissed her cheek and hugged her tightly before passing her to her mother who gave her a hug and sniffled.

"I'm so happy you found your mate, Karly. I wish you a lifetime of happiness and love."

"Thanks, mom." She sniffed.

"Now, you two have to catch the red-eye, so you should probably get going." Her father said with a smile. "We'll drop you off at the airport on our way home."

They gave them the impression that they would wait a little while so they could get dressed, and she and Linus pawed at each other in the bathroom in Jason and Cadence's home and had a really, really fast quickie before they got dressed and said goodbye to everyone.

Once they were at the airport and seated at the terminal waiting to board the plane, Linus kissed the top of her hand. "I'm glad we were able to make love on our wedding night, but I hope you realize that as soon as we get to our hotel that I'm going to take a very...very long time getting reacquainted with my wife in the right way."

"Oh?  What's the right way?" she teased.

He leaned into her ear, "Nice and slow."

*Good.*

As soon as the plane was in the air, she fell asleep against Linus' shoulder, tucked against his side and feeling more blessed than any one person had the right to feel.  Waiting at baggage claim was their driver who was theirs to use for the entire eight days at any time, day or night.

On Goat Island, just a small bridge away from Newport, their suite overlooked the bay, but neither of them was interested in the view out the window.

"Come here, love," Linus said from the bedroom, and she crossed the large sitting room to the lavish bedroom where he lay comfortably posed on the king sized bed.  She kicked off her shoes and climbed up next to him, settling against him on her back as he leaned over to kiss her.  "Did I tell you 'I love you' today?" he whispered against her mouth.

"You might have mentioned it once or twice."  She smiled, sliding her fingers through his thick hair and anchoring him to her mouth.

They kissed for a long time, not stopping until the tug of clothes pulled them apart for mere seconds, and when they were laid bare together, he stretched out next to her and ran his thumb down her jaw.

"I love you, Karly."

"I love you, too, Linus."

"I feel like I didn't really live until I met you.  Like my life was all shadows before and now you're my sun.  I didn't think I'd ever find someone that could love me in spite of everything about me, but you do."

His beautiful blue eyes shimmered with love and contentment. "Because we were made for each other."

They spent the entire day and night of the first day of their honeymoon making love, ordering room service, and driving each other wild. It was absolutely perfect.

The morning of their second day, Linus called for the towncar to take them to First Beach. As requested, the hotel had prepared a breakfast basket for them with coffee and treats to take along. Armed with enough beach luggage for a family of eight, they walked onto the nearly deserted beach and set up their little area as far away from the parking lot and kiddie play structure as they could get and still actually be on the beach.

The large umbrella provided just the right amount of shade for the beach towels that they laid out on top of a sheet they stole from the hotel. Although they had beach chairs set up, they both stretched out on their stomachs and drank coffee and fed each other sliced fruit and chocolate filled croissants, watching the sun glinting off the waves.

Since it was a holiday week, it didn't take long for the beach to fill up, but they were in their own little bubble and ignored everything. After putting on lotion in a nearly obscene way, they walked down into the waves and held hands, walking back and forth along the beach, talking about everything and nothing.

When their stomachs growled for lunch, they ate at a pizza parlor in town and then headed to the hotel to scrub off the sand and play, passing out tangled up, still warm from the sunshine.

She took a bite of heavenly lobster studded macaroni and cheese as they sat on the deck of a restaurant that looked out on the bay and sighed. Now this was bliss. Her husband, a beautiful view, and great food that she didn't have to cook. If they could only be naked, too, that would make it totally perfect.

"Baby?" Linus tapped the end of his fork on the metal table and snapped her from her reverie of watching a boat tour head out into the bay.

"I'm sorry; I was just enjoying the view. What did you say?"

"I said I wanted to talk to you about something important."

She straightened. "Oh, okay. Sure."

He folded his hands after putting his fork on the plate that had held four battered, fried fillets and a huge pile of French fries. "Would you like us to be part of your folks' pack?"

She blinked in surprise. That statement was way out of left field. "I...well, I don't know. What brought this up?"

"Well," he cleared his throat and took a drink of his beer. "It's been bouncing around my mind since our joining ceremony. There's harmony with that pack, a sense of family and belonging that's wholly unique. I know you miss your family, and I'm not so selfish that I would want to keep you from them."

"Who said you were selfish?"

He shrugged. "Me."

She shook her head. "You're not, I promise. Once I knew that no one in my parents' pack would be mine, Linus, I never expected to be part of their pack in any way except as the daughter of a member. If you want to join up with that pack, of course I'll support you, but don't do it for me because I don't need it."

"I just want you to have everything you want and need, sweetheart." He twisted the empty beer bottle in his hand absently.

"I do. I totally have everything I've ever wanted and needed because I have you. I found the missing piece of my heart, and I get to be in your arms forever. So home is wherever we are, in Kentucky or West Virginia...it doesn't matter to me as long as the home includes you."

"But—"

She put her hand up. "Nope. I don't want to take you from your family any more than you want to take me from mine. Besides, your pack needs you. The drive to my parents' isn't so far we that can't visit a few times a year, and they'll come to see us, too."

He looked like he would protest some more or push the issue, so she reached across the small table and took his hand in hers. "There's only one thing that I think is missing from our lives."

"What?"

"A baby."

A slow, sweet smile spread across his face. "Now that's something I can help you with."

"Good. Just know this, love; I'm happier than I've ever been in my life because you're in it."

"Me, too."

* * * * *

It was dark when they walked out of the bar at the hotel and down the winding sidewalk past the small firepit where a few partiers were gathered on wooden lawn chairs chatting. They walked all the way around to the dock at the back of the hotel and pulled a chair into the shadows.

She lifted her skirt as Linus freed his cock from his shorts as he sat on the chair, and she straddled him, sinking down onto his cock and pressing her mouth to his. "Ah, I love you so much, baby," he said, nipping a long line down her neck as she moved slowly up and down his length, the darkness and her long, loose skirt hiding them from any prying eyes.

"I love you, too," she promised, dropping her head to his shoulder and holding him close with one hand tangled in his hair and the other gripping his shoulder. One of his hands dug into her hip tightly, and the other slipped up the front of her tank and under the satin bra. His hand felt warm against the cool evening air, and she leaned back slightly and dropped her head back, closing her eyes and reveling in the sensations coursing through her body.

His hand left her breast and trailed down the front of her body over her clothes before moving under her skirt and gathering her honey on the tips of his fingers and driving her to climax with his fast motions over her swollen bud. She clenched her teeth on the cry in her throat, and it came out a muffled moan that Linus echoed through his own pursed lips, pulling her against him and dampening the sound into her shoulder while his body released into hers.

Panting and drifting down from bliss, he nuzzled against her ear and whispered with a rough voice, "I've never been happier, my sweet angel, and that's the truth."

* * * * *

As is the way of most wonderful things like honeymoons and vacations, they left their little slice of paradise behind, with fond memories of fireworks over the water, the windows wide open at night so they could hear the sounds of the ocean, the siren call of the waves, and having eaten their fill of all things seafood.

She spent the summer full swing in decorating their home. Linus turned one of the two spare bedrooms into a studio for her, surprising her with a top-of-the-line printer and a new lens for one of her cameras. As promised, she took a picture of him in his beautiful shifted form with the woods behind their home as the backdrop, and she was able to get the oil painting finished by his twenty-eighth birthday at the end of July. She surprised him a second time on his birthday with news of her pregnancy. He went into immediate overprotective mate mode and refused to let her near chemicals of any sort except watercolor paints, so she used the photos from their beach trip to make some paintings for the house. They also began to host a Sunday evening meal for the top ranked in the pack.

For the celebration of the anniversary of the near disaster on the day they met, Linus locked them up in the house and turned off all the phones for three solid days so they could enjoy the last bit of bliss of their private time together before their child was born.

In the very early spring, Remy Eugene Mayfield joined their family. Dr. Mirella delivered him at the nearby hospital with hers and Linus' family and his close friends and pack members filling up the waiting room to welcome the next generation of werewolves into the pack.

To look into her baby's gorgeous blue eyes and know that someday he would lead a pack as alpha filled her with pride but also fear; to know the burden of his life as it would come some day. That he'd be responsible not only for his family – his mate and children – but also for the lives of everyone in his pack. Linus was committed to teaching Remy and any other children they had about the history of werewolves.

When Karly turned twenty-one and began her journey to find her wolf mate, she had no idea that the path she chose would take so long to reach the place where she could find rest with her wolf, but she didn't regret the journey. She learned to stand on her own two feet and push on no matter what came at her. To be sure, their lives could have turned out vastly different in many ways, but she was thankful every day when she woke in Linus' arms, in the bed in their home, with their son sleeping quietly in his room.

Once she stared insanity in the eyes and thought she would not live to see another sunrise. Now, she took nothing for granted, especially her family and her husband, who fought for her and never gave up.

Family. Surely this was heaven.

***The End***